EXPELLED F

"What *is* the F.G.?"

EXPELLED FROM ST. MADERN'S

E M Channon

Books to Treasure

Books to Treasure
5 Woodview Terrace,
Nailsea, Bristol, BS48 1AT
UK

www.bookstotreasure.co.uk

First published by Nisbet & Co 1928
This edition 2014

Design and layout © Books to Treasure

ISBN 978-1-909423-13-8

CONTENTS

PREFACE

E M Channon was born Ethel Mary Bredin on 17 October 1875 in Ireland. After her father's death four years later, she and her mother moved to St Leonard's where she attended the Ladies' College. She married Rev Francis Channon in 1904 and together they had six children. Ethel began writing after her marriage and produced numerous books for both children and adults. She is, perhaps, best known for *The Honour of the House*, which was published in 1931, but she wrote another dozen or so stories for girls between 1924 and 1937. She died on 6 June 1941.

EXPELLED FROM ST. MADERN'S

CHAPTER I

LITTLE BLANCHE BATES

"BY the by, darling—did I say that Mrs. Bates is coming to tea today?"

"No, mother," with resignation.

"And—I'm sorry, Dorothy!" Mrs. Grayling's voice shook a little, possibly with amusement; and yet there was something like an apology in the glance which she sent across the room to the sofa.

"Oh, mother! *Not* Blanche too!"

Dorothy gave a little despairing wriggle of head and shoulders—all that she was able to do in the way of remonstrance. For a whole year now, ever since the accident about which she never liked to speak or think, she had passed her life between bed and sofa, lifted from one to the other helplessly like a baby; and the possibility of some day walking again, about which the doctor had prattled hopefully, seemed as far off as ever.

"Yes, Dorothy—I'm afraid so. I couldn't exactly refuse, when her mother begged to bring her. Besides, if she likes coming here so much—"

"It's only piggishness, because she likes your cakes. And she *is* such a little beast!"

"She's rather a miserable little beast, I'm afraid, as spoilt children always are," said Mrs. Grayling. "But they won't stay very long, and—here they are!"

Dorothy made a grimace, and then laughed good-naturedly, and said:

"I'll be good—but don't *press* them to stay when they suggest going!"

"I won't. I really won't!" Mrs. Grayling promised remorsefully.

The door opened, and Dorothy hastily pulled over her feet the light cotton dust-rug that lay on her sofa. She did so hate having remarks made, and she had had experience of Blanche Bates.

"Mrs. Bates and Miss Blanche!" announced Mrs. Grayling's very young housemaid, and she made a private grimace at Dorothy as she retired. She had not had time to learn very much in the three months since she left school; but she was sympathetic—and she too had had experience of Blanche.

"Darling Helen—*too* good of you to have us again so soon!" gushed Mrs. Bates, with a kiss on each cheek. "But I *had* to talk to you. Blanchie, my sweet, come and kiss Mrs. Grayling."

Blanche had been absorbed in a round-eyed consideration of the cakes upon the table. She turned reluctantly, and offered a fat hand with jingling Indian bangles round the wrist.

"*Kiss* Mrs. Grayling, my pet!" her mother urged.

"Certainly not, if she doesn't wish. Some people don't like kissing," Mrs. Grayling responded firmly.

Mrs. Bates was, most certainly, not of that number. She was now fluttering over the sofa where Dorothy lay at her mercy. (You can't dodge when you are lying flat.)

"A little easier to-day, dear?" she cooed.

"I am quite well, thank you," said Dorothy, with dignity. (If *only* people would treat her as though she were like everybody else! And Blanche was coming over, to stare with her round eyes.)

Mercifully, tea came in at that trying moment.

"You haven't got any of those chocolate cakes to-day," Blanche remarked, coming back to stare at her hostess.

"No," said Mrs. Grayling pleasantly.

"*Why* haven't you?"

"Because I made another kind instead."

"Is that cocoa-nut on the top? I don't like cocoa-nut!"

"Perhaps not. But other people do," said Mrs. Grayling, smiling.

"Darling, you'd better *begin* with bread-and-butter. See, so nice and thin!" coaxed Mrs. Bates.

"I don't want bread-and-butter. I want cake!" said Blanche. And, so that there might be no doubt of her meaning, she took a large piece of sponge-cake, and bit into it defiantly.

"*Little beast!*" murmured Dorothy in her mother's ear, accepting her own tea on her own little tray. And, though Mrs. Grayling shook her head reprovingly, she couldn't help smiling in agreement.

"And you really make all these delicious little cakes yourself, Helen? How clever you are!" sighed Mrs. Bates, eating daintily. "How I wish *I* were clever like you!"

"It's the easiest thing in the world—not clever at all," Mrs. Grayling laughed. "Why, Blanche could do it if she tried!"

"Could *she* do it?" Blanche demanded through a mouthful, shaking her head sideways towards the sofa.

"Oh, yes! Dorothy began to learn cooking before she was as old as you."

"Then why didn't she make these?"

(Dorothy wriggled in anguish. She knew exactly what was coming—and it came.)

"Hush, darling!" Mrs. Bates whispered tactfully—and a whisper carries much farther and more distinctly than ordinary speech. "Don't you remember that poor Dorothy is ill, and can't walk or even stand? How *could* she make cakes?"

"Hasn't she got any legs*?*"

"Let me give you some more tea, Cora," said Mrs. Grayling; but in vain.

"Hasn't she *got* any legs?" Blanche demanded stubbornly.

"Oh, thank you, dear Helen! Such a delicious cup—and such a warm day—"

"Hasn't she got any *legs*?"

"Dorothy, you're ready for some more tea, aren't you?" said Mrs. Grayling, rising and going towards the sofa.

"Hasn't she got—?"

"She hasn't got any tea; and you may take her cup back to her," said Mrs. Grayling, filling it.

This seemed an injudicious move, and, indeed, Blanche's mouth was open for a fifth repetition of her question as she reached Dorothy's side; but Mrs. Grayling was one too many for her.

"And then, Blanche, come back for a banana."

She knew the young woman's weakness very well. The obstinate little mouth closed again, and Blanche hurried back to the tea-table.

The bananas had been cunningly hidden until now, and produced while her back was turned: a large, fat bunch, with two specially large specimens on the top.

"You will have one, won't you.?" said Mrs. Grayling superfluously.

"I don't want one: I want two," the young lady answered with firmness, and she stretched out a fat hand to clutch those two of extra size on the top.

"You will not have two in this house," said Mrs. Grayling, with even greater firmness; and she detached the first that came, put it on a plate, and held it out.

("And there," as Dorothy subsequently related the incident to various enchanted friends, "there was the mother looking on, and not saying a word!")

Miss Blanche Bates stared, incredulous; opened her mouth to remonstrate; opened it still wider to roar, while a tear of rage welled into each round blue eye: and then, incredibly, took her plate and sat down and ate her banana in silence. Unlike the proverbial Englishman, she knew when she was beaten.

"Dear Helen, I have quite finished," said Mrs. Bates, in nervous haste. "And—and will you show me anything new that you have in your pretty garden?"

She was making anxious little "faces," as Dorothy said, while she spoke: raising her eyebrows, pursing her lips, nodding her head towards the banana-eater; and Mrs. Grayling took the very broad hint, as she could hardly fail to do.

"Yes, certainly, Cora. But it's very hot still. I must get a hat."

The door closed behind them, and Blanche went on deliberately munching, while Dorothy lay back and closed her eyes. It was too bad! to be left alone with that awful child, and no possibility of escape.

She could feel a question coming. It came.

"Are you asleep?"

"No. But I'm hot and tired."

"Is that why you lie on the sofa all the time?"

Dorothy opened her eyes in despair.

"I lie on a sofa—as you know perfectly well—because I can't walk."

"Why can't you walk? Haven't you got—?"

"I can't walk because I had an accident last year, at my School Sports: in the Long Jump," said Dorothy, with great distinctness.

"Did you break your legs right off?"

"I hurt my back—not my legs."

"Then you *have* got legs!" Blanche proclaimed with triumph.

Dorothy threw off her useless rug with quite a savage movement.

"I've got legs just as much as you have—look and see! But I can't move them. Now you know, and *please* don't ask any more questions!"

She turned her head sharply away, to hide the tears of impatience and misery that had suddenly sprung into her eyes.

There was a silence.

"I—I'm sorry," said a very small voice, quite close.

Dorothy bit her lip and lay still. She wouldn't *let* herself cry.

"Won't you—won't you never be able to walk no more?" asked the small voice; and a fat, soft hand was suddenly slipped into the thin one that hung down from the sofa. There were actually tears in the round eyes that Dorothy turned reluctantly to meet.

"I don't know: nobody knows. The doctor says *perhaps*. I might be able to quite suddenly—and I mightn't for years and years!"

When the two mothers came back, after a rather lengthy interval, they found, with a relieved surprise, silence and peace in the drawing-room. The big girl and the little girl had each a bound volume of *Punch*. The cakes on the tea-table, and the bunch of bananas, were exactly as they had been left.

"Dorothy, I *was* sorry to leave you, and to be so long away; but I really couldn't help myself," Mrs. Grayling apologised, when the visitors had gone.

"It was quite all right. She isn't such a bad little kid, after all," said Dorothy jerkily.

"Poor little thing!" said Mrs. Grayling, beginning to collect cups and saucers in her silent, deft fashion. "She doesn't know it yet; but she's going to school. That was what Mrs. Bates wanted to talk to me about."

"To school!"

"Major Bates is ordered back to India; and, of course, she is too old to go with them. She seems very young for a boarding-school," said Mrs. Grayling compassionately, "and she's young for her age, even, and she has been so spoilt!"

"Where is she going?" asked Dorothy slowly.

"To St. Madern's; you remember, a school that I—went to see once, and liked so much."

"Yes. I remember," said Dorothy, with a muffled voice and her head turned away again. It had not been so very long ago—only last year, just before those disastrous School Sports. There had been some idea that she herself would go away to a boarding-school for the last part of her school career. Mrs. Grayling had come home so pleased with St. Madern's, and everything had seemed delightful and—almost settled. And then Dorothy herself had settled it in quite another way.

And now little Blanche Bates—a spoilt, rather nasty child of not quite eight—was going there, going to have all the pleasures and interests that Dorothy had been looking forward to so much. It was hard—it was *awfully* hard!—and the room was so hot—and she couldn't get out into the garden—

Mrs. Grayling had carried away the tea-tray. She always washed up the china herself, and she would not be back for a good many minutes. Dorothy buried her face in her sofa-cushion, and burst into a flood of despairing tears.

CHAPTER II

A Bit of Slate

IT was a comfort to Dorothy when September was well over: when no one kept coming in to tell her of some gorgeous tennis-party: when everyone—but herself, that is—had gone back to school. The worst bit of all had been the farewell interview with Mrs. Bates, bathed in tears, and Blanche, looking rather scared and solemn.

"Oh, yes, I know it's a very nice school, Helen!" Mrs. Bates sobbed. "The nicest possible school, I'm sure. But—but—"

"And she is so lucky to have her grandmother to go to in the holidays," Mrs. Grayling reminded her comfortingly, thereby very much relieving the mind of Dorothy. (She had had a terrible secret fear—she didn't dare to mention it, for fear of suggesting an idea that perhaps hadn't occurred already after all!—that her too-kind mother might have offered to take the derelict herself; and that would have been beyond words awful.)

"And you will see her sometimes, when she is there, and—and write and tell me—?"

"Of course I will. It's only the next station, you know—no distance at all; and Blanche shall come over to see us every holiday;—shan't she, Dorothy?"

"Yes, rather!" said Dorothy, so relieved at the taking away of that big fear that she could make this small concession quite willingly. Besides, it must be hard to go to school—even to the very nicest of schools—when your father and mother are going away from you hundreds and hundreds of miles across the sea.

"You are both so kind; and I *know* you are fond of her," wept Mrs. Bates, causing Dorothy a secret pang of remorse. And presently the watery visit came to an end; and it was easy to bid quite an affectionate good-bye to a person whom you wouldn't see again for years, and another whom you wouldn't see till the Christmas holidays.

It was easier, too, to lie on a sofa now that the days were beginning to draw in, and the garden was growing uninteresting, and there wasn't any more tennis. The room was snug and cosy when fires began; and Dorothy had determined to work most extraordinarily hard at her lessons this winter, and achieve the most wonderful results before spring came round again. It is very tiring to hold a book when you are lying flat; but she had a reading-stand that did away with this difficulty. Music, of course, was out of the question; and so, almost entirely, was sewing—and Dorothy was a clever needlewoman, and was just beginning to take an interest in making her own frocks. However, lying on a sofa spoils all frocks, and a sort of best dressing-gown is easy to get in and out of, and answers every purpose. Fortunately, Mrs. Grayling had lived abroad a good deal, and spoke two or three languages fluently, so Dorothy got on like a house afire with French and German, and was even acquiring quite a respectable amount of Spanish.

"When I go back to school," she would say bravely, "I shall give Mademoiselle the surprise of her life!" And Mrs. Grayling would answer with a smile, and then make some excuse to turn away and hide her face; for there seemed no improvement in the injured back, and the doctor was beginning to look serious.

"I had hoped for some improvement before this," he told her privately. "If there is not some very definite change for the better before long, I am afraid—"

He didn't finish the sentence; but Mrs. Grayling finished it for him in her own mind without the least difficulty, and went away to her own room and cried most bitterly.

"I'm sure I'm growing ever so much. I shall be too long for the sofa soon—and *then* what will you do?" Dorothy laughed. She was really very brave and good; and she kept her crying fits, when the forlorn reality came over her too unbearably, for bedtime, when they wouldn't disturb her mother. It is dreadfully humiliating to be so tied to a sofa that you can't even go away and wash your face when you want to, to hide the traces of tears.

They got through an immense number of books in those long firelit autumn evenings, Mrs. Grayling reading aloud while Dorothy lay still; or Dorothy reading aloud in her turn, usually French or

German to improve her accent. They played games too, chess and backgammon and piquet. And Dorothy, in the many solitary hours when her mother could not be with her, learnt quantities of poetry by heart, and played more games of Patience than anyone would believe—*anything* that would keep her from thinking about being a prisoner on that sofa. And the wireless was a great comfort; but too much of it tired Dorothy's head, and the doctor did not greatly favour it. And, of course, she had plenty of visitors; but suitable visitors for an invalid are rarer than you might suppose. There were dear elderly ladies who came into the room on tiptoe, and talked to her in almost a whisper, and made her want to scream. And there were other people who said how ill she looked (which annoyed Mrs. Grayling extremely) or how well she looked, "considering" (which annoyed Dorothy even more). And there were school friends who came in bounceably, and talked in voices that sounded very loud in that quiet room, telling of "fearful rags" and "perfect lambs" and things that were "a beastly shame." It seemed to Dorothy, listening, as if she must have been away from school for years instead of months: there were so many changes, and she seemed so out of touch with it all, and so far away. And sometimes, in the middle of an account of a really thrilling hockey match, the speaker would suddenly realise things, and break off in an apologetic hurry—and that was the worst of all. Dorothy did not want to be continually reminded that she had been the fastest forward that had ever played for the school, and the youngest.

There were, of course, just a few people who had either been ill themselves, or who were sympathetic enough to understand just what it felt like to be a sofa-prisoner, and of these Dorothy was never weary. But unfortunately visitors of this sort are so rare and valuable that they are wanted in every direction at once, and find difficulty in fitting anything extra into their already overcrowded days, while the tactless sort are idle people who can spare unlimited time to bore and weary one to death. It is surprising how much you learn about your fellow-creatures when you lie on a sofa and can't get away from them.

So the autumn days went by, not too slowly on the whole. And October, that long but pleasant month, was gone, and November came. And with November came the worst day that Dorothy had yet experienced.

It was one of those days when everything goes wrong from the very beginning. She woke up with her back feeling particularly uncomfortable, so that she longed with all her might to get up and run round and round the room; and, in spite of her usual resolution, a few tears oozed out at the thought that she couldn't. It was raining and foggy, and they had to have the lights turned up for breakfast; and Mrs. Grayling had a particularly busy day in front of her, and a headache—the unpleasantest of combinations. Hetty, the little maid, dropped the whole tray of breakfast things, stumbling over a loose bootlace at the very door; and two plates, a cup and saucer, and the hot-water jug were broken—wonderfully little, considering—and Dorothy jumped on her sofa at the sudden noise, and jarred her back and frightened her mother. The porridge was a little burnt: just little enough to leave it eatable, and just enough to make it distasteful. And the postman had passed their door without leaving anything for anybody, which always feels like an insult.

"*Must* you go out this morning? It's such a horrid day, and I'm sure your head is bad," Dorothy urged as the red-eyed Hetty cleared away the breakfast things with a slow carefulness.

"I can't shirk that committee meeting: it's too important," said Mrs. Grayling with a tired sigh. She was sitting by the fire with some very fine sewing, and she leaned forward at this moment to use the poker rather ineffectually.

"This last load of coal is very bad: so slaty and bad to burn," she said; and she picked up with the tongs several little hard bits that had shot out of the fire all over the hearth.

"Could Mrs. Borch speak to you for a minute, ma'am?" inquired Hetty at the door. And Dorothy said: "Oh, *dear!*" and Mrs. Grayling looked it.

"I must go," she said, and put down her work in a hurry and went out of the room.

Dorothy lay back feeling cross. Things *were* going wrong to-day: mother with a headache and a committee meeting, and now Mrs. Borch, the most tiresome of women, to make the one worse, and probably lead to unpunctuality at the other—and Dorothy would have even a longer piece of the morning quite alone than need otherwise have been. And she was tired of Patience—oh, deadly tired! And she had finished her library book, and her head felt too stupid to learn anything by heart. A forlorn tear trickled out of the corner of each eye, and even that didn't matter; mother would be in too much of a hurry to notice it when she went out.

But things were worse even than this. Mrs. Grayling was so much hindered by the leechlike Mrs. Borch that she hadn't even time to run in and say good-bye and fetch the library book to change. Dorothy could hardly believe her ears when she heard the gate open and close quickly; but Hetty came in a minute after with her lunch, and confirmed the incredible bad news.

"The milk's burnt," said Dorothy, with a little sniff and a wrinkled nose.

"Well, I was afraid it was, miss; but I hoped it wasn't enough for you to notice," said Hetty distressfully.

"Take it away, please. I can't drink it," said Dorothy, and ate biscuits with a very gloomy expression. This was surely the last straw!

The rain was still coming down steadily, though the fog had lightened a little. One could just see to read; but there wasn't anything *to* read. She put out a hand and swung round the revolving bookcase that stood by her, reading all the titles in turn, and she didn't fancy any of them. She could, of course, ring for Hetty and have any other book in the house fetched for her; but—oh, well, Hetty would be sure not to be able to find anything that she really wanted, and she didn't know what she did want, if it came to that. What a long, long time it was since she had been able to go where she liked and choose for herself!

The two herald tears were suddenly followed by quite a flood, and Dorothy lay sobbing on the sofa as if her heart would break. It didn't matter how red she made her eyes and nose. No one was likely to come in this streaming morning, and her mother would not be back for *hours*. The whole of life seemed hateful and miserable and dreary.

There are several points in favour of a real good cry. It is a decided relief to one's feelings: it washes away some of the soreness of heart, and it usually leaves one tired and a little drowsy. After Dorothy had cried as much as she wanted to, which was a good deal, and had dried her red eyes and blown her red nose, she found that she had a bad headache and felt thoroughly tired. And, as there was nothing much to do but fall asleep, she did that.

She dreamt a long and elaborate dream.

She was in Westminster Abbey, going to some service of the greatest pomp and ceremony. There were crowds of people, all gorgeously attired, and all looking full of eagerness and enthusiasm; and Dorothy, for some reason known not even to herself, was wearing an old pair of bedroom slippers, and they preyed upon her mind terribly. She kept among the thickest of the throng, hoping to hide them from everybody; but people kept melting away from her in all directions, so that her feet were distinctly visible. In a place like that, and among perfect strangers, she couldn't have explained, even if she had had any explanation to give, and the embarrassment was awful. And then suddenly somebody said: "They're coming!" and there was a sound of singing and footsteps, and Dorothy found herself and her bedroom slippers in the very front row of all, with every eye upon them. But she herself forgot them almost at once in amazement at the advancing choir, processing very solemnly down the nave of the Abbey. First came tigers, walking two and two very staidly, with all their mouths opening and shutting in perfect regularity as they sang; and behind them came girls in Eastern dress with long flowing black hair, singing also; and the song that they sang, to a beautiful and uncommon tune, was this:

> "Lap the Parker, be benign!
> Lap the Parker, be benign!"

One is very rarely surprised in dreams, and Dorothy took all these things quite as a matter of course. The only thing that really worried her was a fear that she wouldn't remember the tune—that beautiful and uncommon tune—when she woke up. She leaned forward, listening with all her might; and suddenly the Kaiser leaned over her shoulder with a pistol in his hand, and shot straight at the great stained-glass window opposite. What a crash! And Dorothy found herself saying: "Just the sort of thing I should have expected you to do!"

She was saying it quite out loud; and suddenly there was no Abbey, no chanting choir, and—a great relief this—no bedroom slippers. It had all been so real, that for a moment she looked round quite bewildered. She was in the familiar room at home, lying on the too-familiar sofa, looking across at no stained-glass window, but at the cheerful shining fire, with her mother's chair beside it and her white work thrown down as she had left it in her haste.

And something else.

The end of a dream is very often something real: usually a noise. And the noise that had awakened Dorothy must have been the flying out of one of those little bits of slaty coal of which her mother had complained. There was a little black something on the white work, and—oh, horror!—a little licking trail of fire running up from it: up the beautiful white embroidery that was a nearly-finished wedding present.

Dorothy was across the room, with her rug in her hand; and it was such a tiny flame—so easily put out—

"*Dorothy!*"

Not her mother's voice, surely? She had never heard it sound like that before! And yet there was Mrs. Grayling, pausing in the doorway, staring, staring, with such a white face and such unbelieving eyes—and it was only then that Dorothy realised herself to be standing on her two feet, as she had never done for more than a year.

"My dear—my dear child!"

Mrs. Grayling had her by the arm by that time, holding her up; and Dorothy had gone, of a sudden, all weak and trembling. Her legs seemed to have no power left in them, as she sank into the nearest chair: though, even so, it was wonderful to be sitting up, instead of lying flat.

"It was—your lovely work. A bit of coal—" she found herself attempting to stammer out in explanation. And then, to her shame and horror, she began to laugh and cry together, in the most ridiculous way, and couldn't say any more. And her mother had gone away …

But she was back again in half a minute, with something fizzy in a tumbler, which tasted horrible, but made Dorothy feel at once more like her real self, and less like nothing on earth. She looked round her in a dazed fashion; and it *wasn't* a dream. She was actually sitting in her mother's chair by the fire. And she made a vague attempt to move her feet, and they actually *did* move. It was too wonderful.

"Sit still for a minute, darling," said Mrs. Grayling, in the queerest breathless voice. "The doctor will be here directly—I have sent Hetty—"

"Oh, mother—is it *really*—?"

"Dorothy, I really hope so; but we mustn't make too sure," said Mrs. Grayling, with a great sob. "You see—I didn't tell you—but the doctor said—any shock—*might*—"

"I was asleep, and I woke up and saw your work on fire, and I never thought about anything but saving it," Dorothy explained shakily. "Oh, I do hope it isn't much spoilt!"

"My darling child, what does that matter if—if—?"

And then the doctor was there—Hetty must, indeed, have run like the wind—asking questions, and making little experiments, and speaking in a quiet and reassuring voice that was most helpful to rather shattered nerves. And his final verdict was more than either of them had dared to hope.

"Yes. Dorothy may walk again now; and very soon I hope she will be quite like other girls. But she must be careful, and do as she is told, and not be too ambitious, and have massage."

"I'll do anything—*anything*!" Dorothy promised fervently.

"You have been the best of girls," said the doctor, with a kindly pat on her shoulder. "Very good, and very patient, under a very great trial; and I'm nearly as glad as you are that it is over."

"I haven't been good—I haven't been patient," Dorothy stammered with a guilty conscience, struggling against tears.

"Perhaps you are not the best judge of that," the doctor smiled at her. "Now I'll help you out of that chair—gently, gently!—and you can go into the dining-room and have a good luncheon."

What a wonderful thing to do! Not to most of us, of course; but to Dorothy a treat beyond all words delightful. Her feet felt most queerly weak and shaky, and she was very glad of the doctor's arm; but she actually did walk in—across the hall, and in at a door which she had not opened for many months. And she found herself sitting in a room so strange to her that she had to keep looking round and round, seeing and remembering all the little things that she had quite forgotten. And she had no appetite at all; but that was, perhaps, hardly to be wondered at.

CHAPTER III

THE VERY NICE SCHOOL

"OH, I am longing for next term!" Dorothy cried rapturously. "Just fancy that I ever wanted the holidays to be longer than they were! I feel sometimes as if I really can't wait so long as the third week in January."

"Yes, darling," said Mrs. Grayling. She hesitated a minute, and then added: "But—it won't be the High School, Dorothy."

"Not the High School?" Dorothy repeated, and her joyous face became suddenly blank.

"No, dear. You *must* go steadily, you know, for a long time to come; and you certainly couldn't manage cycling there and back, even if it was only once a day—and you know it's often more than that."

"I could stay for dinner—or there's the bus—"

"In any case, there would always be the possibility of getting wet or chilled, and you will not be able to take *any* risks for months to come," said Mrs. Grayling, in a steady voice. "It might mean—the sofa again, you know, Dorothy."

Dorothy gave a little shiver, looking at the inoffensive sofa with aversion.

"Besides," said Mrs. Grayling, pursuing her advantage, "you can't have forgotten that I always meant you to have a year or two away from home before you finished your school-days."

"I'm not sixteen yet!" Dorothy defended herself quickly.

"No. But you will be before next term begins."

There was another little pause, while Dorothy looked out of the window and blinked fast. It *was* a blow: there was no getting over that. Hadn't she and Jessie Vavasour and Kitty Brown and her own particular chum Evelyn spent all the last evening gloating over the delightful prospect of being all together again so soon, in the usual familiar surroundings? It had been a most giggling and happy discussion. She had accepted, of course, the unpleasant facts that she would have to be very careful in heaps of irritating ways, that she mustn't play hockey or dance or drill for the whole of the winter; and that was bad enough. But—not to go back to *school!* to the girls who were her particular friends and enemies, and the lessons she liked or didn't like, and the mistresses who were absolute beasts or the most perfect lambs, and the hundred and one interests of that most interesting place. Of course she had rather looked forward to leaving, sooner or later; but then there would have been all the excitement of a last term, with plans and expectations and vows of everlasting friendship. But now—! Could it be possible that she had actually left without knowing it, robbed unconsciously of all those many thrills? Was her very last appearance as a member of the school the dreadful, hazy afternoon when there were white faces all round her, and her mother's—the whitest of all—bending over her, and she tried so desperately not to scream with the agony in her back as she was carried away from the Games Field? ... Dorothy gave a little shiver. Even now she didn't like to think of that.

But there was her mother now, just across the room, looking at her with wistful eyes—and there *was* reason in what she had said.

Dorothy pulled herself together, swallowed a lump in her throat, and asked gruffly:

"Where am I going, then?"

"To St. Madern's—you remember, I spoke to you about it before—"

"Yes. Where Blanche Bates is!"

"Well—yes," said Mrs. Grayling, with a little falter in her voice. She knew perfectly well that that was no recommendation for St. Madern's; and perhaps, in her secret heart, she repented having told Mrs. Bates of that very nice school.

"It's pretty short notice, and most boarding-schools have waiting-lists yards long!" said Dorothy hopefully.

"I know that. So I said nothing to you until I had written and had an answer. Miss Chilcott has room for you, and will be delighted to have you."

Dorothy swallowed another inconvenient lump, and went on

staring out of the window. She couldn't think of any other obstacle at all, try as she might.

"Then—it's all settled?" she said at last, after a very long pause.

"Well, yes, dear; I think it is."

Mrs. Grayling's voice trailed away rather forlornly, and she looked at Dorothy more wistfully than ever. From her point of view it was going to be a great deal worse for her than for anyone else, because she would be left alone at home, with no new interests to take her thoughts away from the recollection that a term of three months is rather a long time.

"It really is a *very* nice school," she said, after a forlorn little silence.

Dorothy turned round quickly, giving herself a mental shake; it wasn't safe yet to give a physical one. She was not a selfish girl, and the little tremble in her mother's voice had been quite perceptible.

"I'm sure it is, and I expect I shall be awfully happy there—only awfully glad to get back again to you in the holidays, you know!" she said, with a laugh that really did her credit, and a little hug that took away the wistful look from Mrs. Grayling's face altogether. "Now tell me lots more about it!"

"Well, it seems such a long time ago since I was there, and so much has happened since, that I'm not quite sure of everything," said Mrs. Grayling. "It's in a most lovely part, quite in the country, with beautiful bracing air that makes you want to walk and eat all day long! And I've got the prospectus, with pictures of the house and grounds; and Miss Chilcott wants me to go down and see her as soon as I can to talk things over—and after that I shall be able to tell you everything you want to know."

"Oh! That will be very nice!" said Dorothy bravely, trying to speak with conviction.

"I thought perhaps I might manage one day next week; and would you like Evelyn to stay here for the night and keep you company?"

"Oh, that *would* be jolly!" said Dorothy; and this time there was no need to try to pump enthusiasm into her voice. It was, indeed, the happiest of suggestions; and she bade her mother good-bye, when the day came, with entire cheerfulness.

"Remember that Hetty is *very* young. Don't try to make her cook anything that she doesn't understand!" said Mrs. Grayling on the doorstep.

"Oh, no, mother! *I'm* going to cook!" said Dorothy, with importance and confidence, and returned forthwith to the kitchen to put her words into action. ... It was so very jolly of mother to have left all the ordering of meals to her for this twenty-four hours!

Would you like to know the menu that she planned out with such care, and carried out with such triumph? It was simple but charming. Dinner: sausages and mashed potatoes and chocolate éclairs from a shop. Tea: dripping toast, strawberry jam and Devonshire cream, roast chestnuts, and some buns of her own making. Supper: egg sandwiches, cucumber sandwiches, and home-made ices. Breakfast: scrambled eggs, coffee, and brown bread and butter.

"I don't know when I've had such jolly food!" said Evelyn, taking a most reluctant farewell when it was time to start for school. They were both a little sleepy, because they had chatted in bed till the church clock surprised them exceedingly by striking One.

"It can't be that, really!" Evelyn exclaimed in horror, when they both had listened in vain for more strokes that did not come. But Dorothy consulted her luminous-faced watch and found that such was actually the case, and, though they both declared with vehemence that they were anything but sleepy—perhaps a supper of cucumber sandwiches and ices does not make for immediate slumber they were very hard to wake when Hetty thundered at their door some six hours later.

And Mrs. Grayling, meanwhile, had not had quite the happiest of expeditions.

She had gone off cheerfully enough—though with a little undercurrent of sadness, because this all meant preparation for her first real long separation from Dorothy—because even mothers enjoy an occasional little jaunt by themselves, and also she was quite as glad to be free of planning meals for twenty-four hours as Dorothy was to assume that duty. And she had always been fond of Amy Chilcott in their school-days: it would be pleasant to have a quiet evening together recalling old times when the business matters about Dorothy had been fully discussed and settled. Besides, she had not been away from home for even a day since the accident happened, and it was good to see something else besides the little home town and the river and the flat country round rising into mild little hills in the distance.

St. Madern's was in a very different part of the world. You had to go up or down hill to get anywhere, and most of the hills were pretty steep. There was no town within sight, only wide rolling country for miles and miles on every side. And the air was, as she had told Dorothy, something to boast of. Even the whiffs of it that came in at the train windows were refreshing; and, when she stood at last on the little country platform, it made her forget at once that she was tired, and suggested greedily that some tea would be very welcome.

Miss Chilcott was waiting for her, and she had a little car outside which she drove herself.

"It's only a couple of miles, you remember, Helen."

"Yes. I remember quite well, now that I am here again," said Mrs. Grayling, looking round her. "It's good of you to have me, Amy— so much easier to talk things over than to write them."

"I love to have you," said Miss Chilcott.

She had always been something of a gusher when she was a schoolgirl, and the words were just what might have been expected— but the tone wasn't. It was curiously flat and lifeless. It made Mrs. Grayling look at her in surprise, and make an involuntary remark.

"I don't think you are looking at all well, Amy!"

"I'm perfectly well, thank you!" said Miss Chilcott, a little sharply, and began to talk at once of Dorothy. Was she really well again? Would she be able to play games? Oh, what a pity! And what a terrible time Mrs. Grayling must have had, all through the past year!

"So bad, that I don't want to talk about it, please. How very good it is of you to take her at such short notice! I was very much afraid that your numbers might be full."

"I am very glad to be able to take her," said Miss Chilcott, again in that flat and lifeless voice.

"The doctor is most anxious for Dorothy to have special massage," said Mrs. Grayling; "and I was so glad to remember that you had Miss—Marvell, was it?—who was so exceptionally clever in that way."

"Oh! Miss Marvell has left," said Miss Chilcott flatly.

"Left! Oh, I *am* sorry!"

Mrs. Grayling sounded so dismayed that a further explanation seemed necessary.

"Yes. I was sorry, too, for she was very good. But she had a most difficult temper, and there was nothing but trouble with the girls—it was impossible to keep her; and, indeed, she didn't wish to stay."

"She seemed such a nice, clever woman—"

"Oh, yes, she was! But my present games-mistress, Miss Adair, is also a trained masseuse," said Miss Chilcott. "I am sure she will be able to undertake all that you want for Dorothy."

They had been running slowly up a narrow, steep, winding lane; and now Miss Chilcott turned in through tall iron gates, standing open, and went on up an avenue which was also uphill. Mrs. Grayling, looking about her, felt that she had not exaggerated in telling Dorothy that it was a beautiful place. There were tall trees and shaven lawns and well-kept flower-beds. From the distance came an enthusiastic shouting that could only mean a well-contested hockey match. The house, before which they now drew up, was of grey stone, very large, with wide attractive windows. An exceedingly trim maid in a dark green uniform stood waiting to receive them.

"Home will seem very small to Dorothy when she comes back at Easter," Mrs. Grayling thought to herself a little ruefully, with a recollection of willing but untidy little Hetty. And then she smiled, for she knew quite well that to a girl of Dorothy's sort there would never be any place like home.

As they crossed the large hall a girl almost blundered into them, walking with her head down: a small girl with an old face and large round spectacles, and a pile of books under her arm.

"Phyllis!" said Miss Chilcott.

"I—I *beg* your pardon, Miss Chilcott!" the girl stammered, turning a very unbecoming moist pink. "I was putting those new atlases in your room, as you said—"

"No need to walk with your eyes shut, even so!" said Miss Chilcott. She turned to Mrs. Grayling. "This is the Captain of the School, Phyllis Wills."

Mrs. Grayling smiled and shook hands, not enjoying the process at all, for the hand that met hers was damp and hot with shyness.

Miss Chilcott nodded dismissal, and Phyllis blundered away down a side-passage, dropping three books on the way.

"The Captain of the School," Miss Chilcott repeated, with her eyes on Mrs. Grayling's face.

"She is rather—rather *young*, isn't she?" said Mrs. Grayling, hesitating a little as she spoke, for the first adjective that came into her mind was quite different, and not nearly so polite.

"She is nearly eighteen—*much* older than she looks," said Miss Chilcott quickly; "and an *exceedingly* clever girl! She passed the Senior Oxford when she was only fifteen. Her father is Sir Willoughby Wills, the surgeon, of Harley Street."

Mrs. Grayling said: "Oh!" She did not feel that Dorothy would be at all impressed by Phyllis Wills, even with these high recommendations.

Tea was waiting in a delightful drawing-room, large and sunny, looking out on to flower-beds, and a yew hedge and high hills rising up purple in the distance; and Mrs. Grayling was glad of her tea. It was partly because of her journey and the fine clear bracing air; but partly also it was for the pleasure of eating cakes that she had not made herself, and drinking out of dainty china that she would not have to wash up herself presently, rather than trust it to Hetty's clumsy red fingers.

"By the way, I forgot to ask you—how is little Blanche Bates getting on?"

"Oh, quite well, I think," said Miss Chilcott, in a voice that was flat and uninterested.

"Does she give you much trouble?"

"Oh, *no!* A very quiet child."

"You must have reformed her wonderfully, then; for that was not at all her reputation with us!" said Mrs. Grayling, with a surprised laugh.

"A *very* quiet child," Miss Chilcott repeated. "In fact, we think her rather dull."

"I brought some chocolates for her. I suppose you don't mind?"

"I'm so sorry, Helen; but we only allow sweets on Sundays. But give them to me—how good of you to bring them!—and I'll see, of course, that she has them."

Mrs. Grayling looked a little disappointed.

"I'm *so* sorry," Miss Chilcott repeated. "But there were so many bothers with hampers and things that were sent and bedroom parties—which, of course, we *can't* have—and people getting knocked up. So I had to make a definite rule and keep to it."

"Poor Blanche! She has such a very sweet tooth—but I'm sure the rule is wise, and perhaps specially good for her," said Mrs. Grayling, rather ruefully. She was thinking, as a matter of fact, not nearly so much of Blanche as of her own cherished plan of sending Dorothy to school nobly equipped with a hamper of home-made luxuries.

"You'll let me see Blanche presently?" she suggested. "Her mother will so love to have a personal assurance that she is happy and all right."

"Oh, of course! In fact, you'll see the whole school at supper—you don't mind, do you?" said Miss Chilcott. "I have tea alone for a little breathing-space; but the rest of the meals we have all together."

Mrs. Grayling answered quite truthfully that she did not mind at all. She was, in fact, most anxious to see all these girls who were going to be companions for Dorothy.

The big dining-room was another very pleasant room with another delightful view; and Mrs. Grayling was quick to notice, when she came downstairs presently from her pretty room for supper, that the china and other things on the table were just as attractive in their way as Miss Chilcott's own private tea-table. There were three long tables, and the girls, in their pretty green uniforms, stood at attention behind their chairs, waiting for Grace to be said. Mrs. Grayling had already been introduced to all the assistant mistresses, and she was now doing her very best to remember which was which. It would add so greatly to the interest of Dorothy's letters if her mother could remember for herself that Miss Pember (reported a perfect beast) was the little dark thing with glasses, or that Miss Tuke (reported the most absolute lamb) was the very young tall girl with red hair.

The supper was very nice—rissoles and stewed fruit and junket—and the manners of the school were beautiful. It was only natural, of course, that a good many glances of polite interest should be cast at Mrs. Grayling, who was unlucky on this occasion in having a very shy girl sitting next to her. On her previous visit, her neighbour had been a chatterbox and conversation had flowed freely; but to-day it was very uphill work. Perhaps both parties were equally relieved when the meal was over.

"Blanche!" said Miss Chilcott.

"Yes, Miss Chilcott!"

Mrs. Grayling found suddenly, with remorseful surprise, that she had forgotten the existence of Blanche altogether. She had been so very busy in committing to memory all those items that she would be so glad to know when Dorothy had come here and she herself was alone at home.

"Come into the drawing-room and talk to Mrs. Grayling."

"Yes, Miss Chilcott!"

It was Blanche's little piping voice, without any doubt; but otherwise Mrs. Grayling was not at all sure that she would have known the meek and demure person in the green uniform, following so obediently in their wake. Miss Chilcott turned off in some other direction at the drawing-room door, leaving them tactfully to have their talk alone.

"Well, Blanche, it's nice to see you again," said Mrs. Grayling kindly. "And I think you've grown! I shall tell your mother so when I write."

"Yes, Mrs. Grayling!"

"Are you happy here, my dear?"

"Yes, thank you, Mrs. Grayling."

"Do you like the games?"

"Yes, thank you, Mrs. Grayling."

"And the lessons? Are you getting on well?"

"Yes, I think so, Mrs. Grayling."

It was awful: like an old-fashioned lesson-book, with question and answer. And it was so unlike the old Blanche! Mrs. Grayling felt hopelessly at a loss; but she tried one more tack.

"Have you made any special friend among the girls?"

This time the answer was not so ready: in fact, no answer came at all. Blanche looked quickly up with the oddest glance, as if she wanted to say whatever was expected of her, and could not make out what that might be, and then she sat silent. Mrs. Grayling looked at her attentively, for at the back of her mind, all this time, was the disturbing thought of that letter that had to go to India. What could truthfully be said in it? The child had certainly grown, and she looked well fed and well cared for; her little fuzz of yellow curls was as neat as a new pin.

"Your hair looks very nice. Do you do it yourself?"

"No, Mrs. Grayling."

"Who does it then?"

"One of the big girls: Rita Salmon."

"That is very kind of her!"

"Yes, Mrs. Grayling."

"Perhaps the big girls all help the little girls in that way?" Mrs. Grayling suggested.

"Yes, Mrs. Grayling."

"That is very kind of them," said Mrs. Grayling, rather weakly. They seemed to have come to a full-stop again.

"Yes, Mrs. Grayling."

"I brought you some chocolates; but Miss Chilcott tells me that she only allows them on Sundays, so she is keeping them for you till then."

"Thank you, Mrs Grayling!"

There was a very little look of the old Blanche in the round blue eyes at that point, and the thanks were not quite so wooden. Mrs. Grayling was encouraged to go on.

"Did Miss Chilcott tell you that Dorothy is coming here after Christmas?"

"Yes, Mrs. Grayling."

"You will be glad to have someone you know, won't you?"

"Yes, Mrs. Grayling."

What *was* the matter with the child? If it hadn't seemed preposterous, one might almost have fancied that she looked frightened at the idea of Dorothy's coming: certainly she was not "glad" in any real sense of the word.

"My dear, *what is it?*" Mrs. Grayling asked impulsively, taking a small hand that was rather cold. "What is the matter with you? You are not one little bit like the old Blanche!"

But no—there was "nothing the matter." Blanche was "quite happy." She had "nothing to tell." And Mrs. Grayling, after several vain endeavours, had to fall back on just ordinary home news. She told of Dorothy's wonderful recovery, and how much she was now able to do like other people, and how after a time she would be just her old self again; and Blanche listened quite politely and patiently, making appropriate rejoinders—and you might as well have talked to a wooden child. It was a real relief to Mrs. Grayling when Miss Chilcott came in.

"Blanche, I'm afraid you must go to bed now."

"Yes, Miss Chilcott!" and she went off with an instant and perfect obedience that was beyond all praise.

"Well—you've had your talk!" said Miss Chilcott, moving rather restlessly about the room. She paused a moment, as if listening, and then laughed suddenly.

"Do you hear that?" she asked.

"The piano, do you mean?" said Mrs. Grayling.

"Yes!"

Mrs. Grayling became all at once aware that she had, in a vague sort of fashion, heard a piano going on and on all this time, while she talked to Blanche. There was nothing so very remarkable in that in a girls' school, though it was certainly late for practising; but it was only one small tune being played over and over again, and that a hymn-tune.

"That's for your benefit!" said Miss Chilcott, laughing again.

"For *my* benefit?" Mrs. Grayling asked, puzzled.

"Yes! The big girls take it in turns to play the hymn at prayers in the morning, and it happens to be the turn to-morrow of poor Gwen Rivers, who is far from musical. She came to me in great agitation just now to ask if 'she'—that's you, Helen!—would come in to prayers to-morrow, and went off with a face of despair on hearing that you certainly would. That's the easiest hymn in the book, and she's been practising it ever since! I must really go and send her to bed."

She went out of the room, and presently the despairing tinkle ceased and she came back again.

"Well—you've had your talk with Blanche!" she said again.

It must have been fancy that she was rather breathless—perhaps she had had to run upstairs to stop the musician; but she was certainly looking at Mrs. Grayling with a curious intentness.

"Yes, Amy. It was kind of you to give us such a long time to ourselves."

"I hope you think she does us credit?"

"She looks well, and she has grown," said Mrs. Grayling, hesitating a little. "She—is very quiet: not at all the sort of child that she used to be."

"You noticed a change in her, then?" said Miss Chilcott sharply.

"Well, yes, Amy. I must confess that I did."

Miss Chilcott paused suddenly in her restless moving about the room, put her hands up to her face like a child, and burst into tears.

"My dear Amy! What *is* the matter?" asked Mrs. Grayling, rising and going to her.

"That's just it—I don't know!" sobbed Miss Chilcott. "Helen, there's something wrong with the school—and I don't know what it is!"

CHAPTER IV

"I'll Kill Your Old School!"

"TELL me all about it," Mrs. Grayling suggested comfortingly, when Miss Chilcott had had her cry out and was sitting looking forlornly into the fire.

"That's just the trouble, Helen. If only I *could* tell you! But I don't know what's the matter, and I can't find out."

"How long has it been going on?"

"I don't know. No, that's not true! It's been going on almost ever since I expelled Anita Lyon."

"Why was that?" Mrs. Grayling inquired seriously, a little startled. She was fond of Miss Chilcott and very sorry indeed for her present trouble; but she had to think of her own Dorothy first and foremost.

Miss Chilcott turned round from the fire suddenly and impulsively.

"I had such good luck when I started the school! I got this delightful house—just what I wanted—much cheaper than I had ever expected, and I had no difficulty at all about getting girls and just the mistresses I wanted. *You* know how nice things were, when you came to see me before."

"Yes, indeed! I liked it all immensely," said Mrs. Grayling.

"Everything went splendidly, and I had quite a long waiting-list of girls who wanted to come—wonderful, for such a new school. They were such nice girls, too, and one or two really clever, who went in for quite good outside exams. and passed well, and of course that did the school more good than anything. Everything seemed happy and jolly too: almost like a very big family. But I suppose even the nicest family has its black sheep, and ours was Anita Lyon."

"What was wrong with her?"

"Just a really naughty girl: naughty on purpose, I mean. Nothing so terribly bad: just breaking rules and being defiant and making other girls misbehave out of impishness. She was clever—one of our exam. successes—and amusing and afraid of nothing: the sort of girl whom other girls admire enormously and take a pride in imitating. And I daresay, perhaps, I was impatient; but I think perhaps patience is the last virtue one learns!"

Miss Chilcott gave a little laugh that was not at all merry.

"Miss Marvell, the games-mistress—the one you liked—couldn't bear Anita. She was a splendid mistress in everything but her temper, but that was very bad. Anita found it out at once, of course, and seemed to take a pleasure in annoying her. It wasn't difficult to do, at the best of times; but Anita had all sorts of impish tricks that would have tried the patience of a saint—and Miss Marvell wasn't that. I needn't bother you with the final details; but Anita played one last trick that went beyond bounds, and Miss Marvell came to me in a flaming rage and said that she was going to leave immediately. She had never been so insulted in her life and she wouldn't stand it for another day."

Mrs. Grayling gave a sympathetic murmur.

"Yes, it was horrible for me! I didn't *want* to lose her—I knew I should never get anyone half so good—and I said everything I could think of to calm her down. But it was all no use, even though I offered to send Anita away at once. Miss Marvell went upstairs and packed, and came down and went straight away with just a little suit-case, walking to the station. She was too furious even to let me drive her in the car. And there was I left, with no games-mistress and half the term still to run!

"I came back from setting her off at the gate—she wouldn't even shake hands with me—and was met at the door by the cook, red with rage. Somebody had slipped into the kitchen and hidden all her frying-pans, and she hadn't found it out till just as she wanted to use them. Of course none of the girls are ever supposed to go near the kitchen; but nobody had the slightest doubt who had done it. I don't think I have a very bad temper myself, Helen, but I confess that I lost it altogether at that point. I was very much upset already, about Miss Marvell, and this seemed the last straw. I sent for Anita, told her what I thought of her, and expelled her on the spot."

"How did she take that?" Mrs. Grayling inquired.

"She simply couldn't believe her ears—I believe she really

thought we were all too much afraid of her to do anything really serious: she was so much admired by the girls, and she had done so well in her exam., and her father was so immensely rich. All she said was, staring at me: 'You don't *mean* that, Miss Chilcott, of course! You'll think better of it, when you've got your temper back!'"

"What impertinence!" said Mrs. Grayling.

"Oh, impertinence! We were all well used to that, from her," said Miss Chilcott passively. "She'd never gone quite so far before, of course; and it didn't make me any more inclined to unsay what I'd said, and gradually she began to believe it.

"'But I don't *want* to go!' she said.

"'You should have thought of that before,' I told her.

"'Well—you'll let me stay the rest of the term, of course?'

"'*No*,' I said. I was quite determined about that. She was too clever and too dangerous. I wasn't going to run any more risks.

"'Well—at least you'll let my father write and say that he wants me to leave at once?' she said.

"'*No*,' I said again. 'You've gone too far for that, Anita. I've put up with you for far too long already, and I'm not going to save your face now.'

"'You're not really going to expel me!' she said, as if she hadn't really believed it, even yet. And I said 'Yes.' I was still angry enough to enjoy saying it.

"She stood staring at me for a couple of minutes, turning quite white; and then suddenly she almost *spat* at me.

"'Very well, I'll go! *But I'll kill your old school!*'"

"What a dreadful girl!" exclaimed Mrs. Grayling.

"Oh, she *was*," agreed Miss Chilcott, with a little reminiscent shudder. "She went straight up to her room and locked herself in; and I telegraphed for her father. He came that very afternoon in a huge Rolls-Royce and took her away. Oh, it was awful! I don't know whether he was more furious with me or with Anita; and she never spoke a word to anybody. When they were gone, I went straight to bed and stayed there for a week, really ill; and I don't think I've ever been quite the same since—my nerves, I mean."

"I don't wonder," Mrs. Grayling sympathised.

"Were things easier, when that dreadful girl was fairly gone?"

"Oh, the rest of the term was quite wonderful! I am extraordinarily lucky, you know, in having such a second-in-command as Miss Pember. She took over everything while I was ill, and wouldn't let me hear a word about anything; and when I came back to work again, I found everything running on oiled wheels—*such* peace. Any of the girls who had been a little tiresome before were scared and behaving like lambs; and Miss Pember had even found another games-mistress at once—Miss Adair, who is here still."

"Did you ever hear any more of Anita?"

"Never, since the day she left."

"Well—that was what you wanted, wasn't it?" said Mrs. Grayling, a little puzzled; for Miss Chilcott's face, instead of brightening as she gave that satisfactory answer, grew more and more sad and depressed. She turned impulsively, lowering her voice, though there was no one to overhear.

"My dear Helen—if I didn't know that you would laugh at me, I should say that the girl was a witch, and had *overlooked* the school!"

"Really, Amy!" remonstrated Mrs. Grayling.

"Yes. I know it's silly. I told you that my nerves had never been the same since I was ill after she left. But, since she left, *nothing* has gone right."

"I thought you said that there was perfect peace?"

"Yes, just for the rest of that term. But things began to go wrong in the holidays; and they've gone wrong ever since!"

"What sort of things?" asked Mrs. Grayling gravely, with the thought of Dorothy at the back of her mind.

"Oh, everything!" Miss Chilcott answered, vaguely and hopelessly. "I told you that I had quite a wonderful waiting-list, for a newish school; so it didn't matter much that three girls left unexpectedly at the end of the term—I don't know why. Of course one's never sure of being told the *real* reason. They had all been great admirers of Anita's; but I daresay I should have thought nothing of that, in a general way. Then two of the servants left. Then we had quite a bad outbreak of measles—"

"Well, *that* couldn't be Anita's doing, at any rate!" said Mrs. Grayling.

"No. I suppose not," said Miss Chilcott limply.

Mrs. Grayling looked at her with attention.

"My dear Amy, you *must not* let yourself worry in this perfectly absurd way!" she said, as if they had been back in the old days when she was Head of the School and Amy Chilcott was a delicate little girl in the Fourth. "Do, *do* put the girl out of your mind altogether. She's gone and done with; and it is quite impossible that she should have any further influence on the school."

"You really think so?"

"I'm sure of it!" Mrs. Grayling replied, with energy.

"Yes. Miss Pember says so too. And I know I am foolish," Miss Chilcott agreed meekly. "But—but—Helen, there's something wrong with the school, and I can't make out what it is!"

"You said that before," Mrs. Grayling reminded her gently. "What sort of something?"

"I don't know—I don't know! It's more the *feeling* of the school than anything that actually happens: a sort of knowledge that something is working against me all the time, and I can't put my finger on it. The old jolly feeling of all working together is quite gone. The girls don't *look* as they used to. I often find that they stop talking when I come into a room unexpectedly and look queer—not all of them. It's just one here and there: not one Form, or just the little girls, or just the big girls. In that case, I think I could deal with it better. But it's just isolated girls, scattered up and down the school, who seem to be quite different from the rest; and yet they aren't particularly like each other in work or tastes or anything. You saw the change in little Blanche Bates for yourself."

"Is *she* one of the suspicious ones?" asked Mrs. Grayling, rather startled.

"Oh, yes!" Miss Chilcott agreed, as a matter of course. "But I don't know what is the matter with her and I can't find out. And it's just the same with the others."

"But Blanche, of course, came here long after Anita left?"

"Oh, yes, but that makes no difference at all! So did most of the others."

"Do you know if anyone corresponds with Anita?"

"No. I'm certain about that; for I see all the addressed envelopes, though I don't often ask to read anything. And all outsiders' letters must be sent through parents."

"Then, my dear Amy, you must see for yourself that Anita cannot have *anything* to do with this trouble!"

"She said she'd kill the school, and something *is* killing it," Miss Chilcott murmured, with a weak persistence.

Mrs Grayling looked at her, and again the doubt about Dorothy rose uncomfortably in her mind. Was this at all the sort of school where she ought to be sent? Was this at all the sort of headmistress that would be best for her? Amy Chilcott had always been a gentle, mild-tempered girl; but—not like this!

"Come in!" said Miss Chilcott to a knock at the door, and Miss Pember walked briskly in with apologies—little dark Miss Pember, to whom Mrs. Grayling had been introduced at supper. She had some important problem to lay before Miss Chilcott for instant solution, and in two minutes the problem was solved—but by Miss Pember, though the general impression left upon the minds of all was that Miss Chilcott alone had borne the responsibility. It was most cleverly done; and Mrs. Grayling found herself suddenly obliged to look at things in general from quite a different angle. It was quite evident that the real authority in the school was Miss Pember, and that she was intensely capable; it was equally evident that Miss Pember was entirely devoted to Miss Chilcott and quite content to be, herself, only the power behind the throne.

"I don't know what I should do without her!" Miss Chilcott murmured gratefully, when she had gone; and Mrs. Grayling was so entirely of the same opinion that she found it difficult to reply suitably.

"Can't *she* solve this difficulty for you?" she suggested hopefully; for indeed Miss Pember gave the impression of being a person before whom all difficulties would melt away automatically.

"No. Even she is entirely puzzled!" said Miss Chilcott.

"Can't your Sixth Form find out anything?"

"I think a different sort of Captain might, perhaps. But Phyllis is—rather a weakling, and they don't take any notice of her. Besides, her head is always buried in a book, and she would be the last person in the school to discover anything that was going on."

"What about the others?"

"It's a very small Sixth Form at the moment—only five girls besides Phyllis. Yes, the numbers are going down and down. I've no waiting-list now. A year ago I couldn't possibly have taken your Dorothy."

"How about the other five?" Mrs. Grayling asked, gravely and gently.

"Gwen Rivers is a nice duffer: had to strain every nerve to pass the Oxford, and is quite used to everyone making fun of her mistakes. Rita Salmon is a heavy, slow girl, not at all interesting, but very nice with the little ones in the school. Celia Tanner is terribly delicate: good at games and a clever girl, but she is always knocking up and having to go to bed. Kitty Halliday is a noisy, boisterous sort of creature: very well-meaning, but quite tactless, and the last person in the world to take into confidence over a matter like this. Effie Purcell is a music-maniac, really caring for nothing beyond her piano. She is only in the Sixth at all because she is so old—nearly nineteen."

Miss Chilcott made a little pause and then added sadly:

"You see, not one of these is the sort of girl who is likely to be of any help!"

Mrs. Grayling said nothing; and the clock struck ten.

"What a shame of me, Helen," said Miss Chilcott in quite another voice, "to take up the whole of our only evening with my woes! I meant to have had such a splendid chat over old times. But you can't think what a relief it is to talk it all out; and, besides, I really didn't like to let you send Dorothy here without knowing all about this unpleasantness. You—perhaps you would rather not send her at all?"

Her tone was pathetic, and her eyes were wistful and anxious; and Mrs. Grayling felt guilty—for that was very much what *had* been in her mind.

"Dorothy isn't the sort of girl to set the Thames on fire, you know," she said. "She was really good at games; but of course they are out of the question now—for the present, at any rate. As regards lessons, she's good at languages; but otherwise she is just the ordinary average girl."

Miss Chilcott gave a very mournful little laugh. "In fact—you'd rather send her somewhere else," she said. "And you are trying to soften the blow, in the kindness of your heart, by making me believe that I shouldn't miss much in not having her!"

This was so true, that Mrs. Grayling could not find any answer to it. She felt her colour rising; and her heart smote her as she looked at her old schoolfellow sitting opposite, so anxious and unhappy. After all, Dorothy must meet good and evil wherever she went, and learn to fight her own battles. Perhaps it was cowardly to think of shirking this one for her: after all, Miss Pember, though she wasn't headmistress, was evidently a tower of strength. Perhaps—

"If only I had *one* girl whom I was quite sure of being able to trust—!" said Miss Chilcott, with a long sigh. "Then, perhaps, you wouldn't mind so much—"

Mrs. Grayling all of a sudden unmade her mind entirely, and made it up again.

"You shall have a girl whom you can trust," she said. "You shall have Dorothy. She isn't an Admirable Crichton; but she is absolutely and entirely *straight*."

CHAPTER V

The F.G.

"HOW was Blanche?" asked Dorothy.

"Much quieter," said Mrs. Grayling.

"Well, that's a good thing, at any rate!"

But Mrs. Grayling did not respond to this at all. Indeed, she had responded so little to all the questions showered upon her since her return that Dorothy was much disappointed and felt defrauded.

"You promised to tell me *everything* after you'd been back to St. Madern's and refreshed your memory!" she exclaimed. "And you've told me hardly anything at all!"

"Well—you've seen the pictures of the place, you see—"

"I don't care half so much about the place. I want to hear about the *people*."

"Dorothy, that's exactly what I'm not going to tell you," said Mrs. Grayling, taking a sudden resolution. "You and I can't possibly look at things with the same eyes, and still less at people. You may think a girl or a mistress perfectly delightful, while to me she is absolutely uninteresting—or just the opposite. I *did* say I would tell you anything you asked; but I've changed my mind, because I don't want to prejudice you either way. You had better go and take all your own impressions for yourself. Miss Chilcott is most anxious to have you there, and I'm sure it won't be her fault if you aren't happy."

"Did you tell her what a duffer I am at maths.?"

"I told her everything that I thought she ought to know about you!" laughed Mrs. Grayling. "And she *still* wanted to have you!"

"Then—wouldn't it be fair, as you told her so much, to tell *me* something about *her!*" Dorothy suggested ingeniously.

Mrs. Grayling pondered for a minute or two.

"I haven't seen a great deal of her since I left school, Dorothy, and that is a long time ago. Still, it didn't seem to me that she was very greatly changed. She always was a most gentle, lovable creature, not very well fitted for fighting her own battles: the sort of person whom any generous person would be ashamed to take advantage of."

She gave a half-glance at Dorothy as she spoke, and saw with satisfaction that that shot had gone home. There was never a more generous girl than Dorothy, or one more ready to fight for the weaker side in a quarrel.

"Not a very head-mistressy sort of person, is it, mother?" the girl commented shrewdly.

"No, Dorothy, you're quite right; and I was surprised when I heard that she had started a school. But she is very clever, and she always got on extremely well with other girls. In a school where things went smoothly there is every reason to suppose that she would do very well indeed."

"And if they didn't go smoothly it would be everyone else's job to back her up? *I* see!" said Dorothy, with an understanding nod.

How strongly Mrs. Grayling was tempted to give away the secret that things were *not* going smoothly, and that poor gentle Miss Chilcott was in sore need of being backed up! But she resisted the temptation and said nothing. She would let her one and only Dorothy go in ignorance, and make her own discoveries and fight her own battles. After all, it was only what every other girl must do who went to St. Madern's, and it seemed to her hardly fair that she should take advantage of her own private knowledge. And, besides, it was hardly worth calling knowledge at that! Just Miss Chilcott's nervous statement that there was "something wrong with the school;" and Amy Chilcott had always been a fanciful and imaginative person— and she was very obviously extremely upset by the horrid ordeal of expelling an unsatisfactory girl.

So Dorothy's preparations were made in a spirit of cheerful ignorance. Her uniform was made and her boxes were packed, and a thousand and one necessary little things bought—for it costs a great deal more to fit out a girl for a boarding-school than to send her as a day-girl, when all sorts of ingenious bits of mending and washing can be done at home. And Mrs. Grayling had held to her heroic resolution, and said nothing more than the usual general warnings about nice girls and nasty girls, and whatever is said—or ought to be said—to every girl who goes right away from home for the first time.

"Yes, I *know*, mother darling; and I promise you I won't forget."

And so the day of departure really came, and Mrs. Grayling returned from the station alone. And if she went up to Dorothy's empty room—so unnaturally tidy—and cried a little and said a very earnest little prayer, Hetty was certainly not aware of it, and there was no one else in the house to know. It seemed a very empty house that night, as Mrs. Grayling sat by the fire with her embroidery, casting an occasional little sad glance at the sofa where Dorothy had lain for so many weary months—and could almost have found it in her sore heart to wish that she was lying there again.

As for Dorothy herself, she had started off in the best of spirits: sorry to leave home, of course, but immensely looking forward to the new world of school. She had hardly got used, even yet, to the joy of being able to go about like other people. All the ordinary walking and moving about, and even the very common interest of getting up and sitting down by herself were still quite attractive novelties; and travelling entirely by herself was something really new. She had been too young to do much of that sort of thing before her accident; but here she was now, sixteen, and going alone to the big Junction some fifty miles off, where the St. Madern's girls were accustomed to meet and go on together. Most of them were met at the London station and personally conducted by one of the mistresses; but there were other stragglers, like Dorothy, who came from here and there by cross-country routes.

The proud independence of travelling alone was very agreeable; and she reflected complacently upon the tactfulness of the relations who had sent a Christmas invitation to little Blanche Bates, for otherwise she and Dorothy must inevitably have come together. It was a fresh and sunny January morning, not too cold; and that was a good thing, for there would be half an hour to wait at the Junction for the London train.

Though an important Junction, it is a singularly uninteresting, lifeless place. The wind whistles through it when there is a wind: the rain drenches it when there is rain: the sun beats mercilessly down on it when the day is fine. The waiting-room is of the kind that makes you prefer to wait anywhere else: and there is no bookstall.

Dorothy got out of her carriage with a rather fast-beating heart, and was—glad or sorry? she couldn't have told which—to see another girl with a St. Madern's hat sitting on a seat reading a book. There seemed to be only two other seats, and they were full; so Dorothy sat down by the other girl—at a respectful distance, for she had observed the distinguished little silk hat-cord which, she knew, meant Sixth Form. It was not for her to intrude upon this exalted stranger; but, after all, she couldn't walk up and down the platform for half an hour by herself.

The other girl read on, turning three pages without looking up, and Dorothy had never felt so small in her life. It looked rather a stodgy and learned book: apparently an odd volume of *Natural History*, about Fish and Reptiles; and Dorothy felt shy of producing the frivolous story-book that she herself had been reading in the train. First impressions are so important! and, if it was the custom for St. Madern's girls to read something instructive on their way back to school, it would never do for a new girl to do otherwise.

It was colder than she thought sitting there, and she wished that she had strength of mind enough to get up and begin walking up and down to get warm again—but it was easier to sit still. The London train must come in before long surely; and she looked at her wrist-watch and was dismayed to find that she had only been sitting there five minutes. It seemed like half a lifetime. She opened her handbag and looked carefully over all the things in it; but that didn't take long. And then she stared anxiously at her luggage, sitting by itself on a truck and looking quite as lonely as she felt; and she hoped that it was exactly like all the luggage of all the other girls.

"What is your name?"

Her neighbour had spoken at last, and Dorothy started violently as she turned to answer.

"How do you spell it?"

Dorothy spelt it; and then was sure, with dismay, that she had in some unaccountable fashion committed herself for ever. For her neighbour very deliberately opened her book again, looked up something in the index, and began to read once more. ... It was awful: far more awful than her first silence, when she had merely appeared to be unaware that anyone else was on the seat at all.

There was another interminable pause, while Dorothy wondered despairingly if it wouldn't be possible to take the next train home again, before the London train came in. The silence was broken by an incredible suggestion.

"Would you like to join the F.G.?"

"The—the *what?*" Dorothy stammered.

"The F.G. Our Secret Society at St. Madern's."

"I—I should *love* to," Dorothy answered, with all her heart.

"Well, you can come and talk to me about it to-night in my room. I can't tell you now. Don't talk about it to other people, you know."

"Of *course* not!"

The Sixth Form girl was not nearly so tall as Dorothy, though she looked old. She had thick black hair plaited in a tight pigtail, and slow black eyes without any expression, and a slow, heavy voice.

"The F.G. is only for a few people: just the ones that are suitable," she went on explaining, with great deliberation; and Dorothy felt as flattered as if the Queen had shaken hands with her. So she *had* given satisfaction after all! or she certainly wouldn't have received this thrilling invitation. And presumably her neighbour hadn't been so engrossed in her book as she had appeared to be, but had been taking a quiet observation with the slow black eyes from behind it. For Dorothy hadn't given any information about herself except her name! It was immensely cheering.

"The London train's signalled," said the Sixth Form girl.

Ten minutes ago Dorothy would have found it hard to bear the information. Now, though her heart certainly beat very fast, she was filled with an excited expectation that was almost pleasure. She had begun unbelievably well, and that was half the battle.

The London train rolled in and girls of all sorts immediately rolled out of it—no! that is not the word. They jumped out of it, chattered out of it, laughed out of it: all except one or two people of great dignity with Sixth Form hat-cords, who stepped out at their leisure and surveyed the world with condescending eyes. One person there was also who combined these two modes of arrival. She wore her hat-cord with a difference, and she shrieked and chattered with the youngest of them.

"Hullo, Rita!" she screamed, catching sight of Dorothy's companion. "Had decent hols.?"

"*Mais Kittay, Kittay! Pas si fort!*" came an agitated remonstrance from the unfortunate mistress who had acted as escort. She was a little thin Frenchwoman, and she appeared considerably exhausted.

"Oh, all right, Ma'mselle! But there's nobody here but us! Who's that with you, Rita? Somebody new? What's her name? I say, you're most awfully tall! How old are you? Only sixteen—oh, *lor!*"

Dorothy was not afraid of the exuberant Kitty, who seemed to be a harmless, noisy, good-natured creature; but she was distinctly sorry for Mademoiselle, who toiled after her in vain, bleating remonstrances, like Panting Time in the poem. Kitty took not the least notice of her. She had a thousand things to say in all directions, and she said them all at the top of her voice. She did not mind in the least about the country people scattered about the platform, who listened and laughed and edged a little nearer to hear the cheerful young lady. Dorothy would willingly have listened too, hoping to pick up knowledge that might be useful to her hereafter; but she was diverted by a very small voice at her elbow.

"How do you do, Dorothy?"

It was Blanche; but what a changed Blanche! A little demure, mouse-like creature, who spoke in a decorous undervoice, like that strange ideal child who is seen and not heard. Dorothy felt her own voice to be quite unsuitably loud as she returned the greeting.

"Why, I haven't seen you since the summer, Blanche. How you have—have grown!"

Dorothy hoped that her hesitation before the last word was not so perceptible to Blanche as to herself; for it wasn't nearly so much the fact of her being bigger that was so noticeable as her quietness and the odd little strained look on her face. Was she being too hard-worked at her lessons? Dorothy wondered. She had, of course, like the usual spoilt child, done hardly any at all while her mother was in England. Probably she *had* had to work hard to catch up with other little girls of her age.

"Did you have nice holidays?"

"Yes, thank you, Dorothy," said Blanche, with perfect propriety; and then she faded away as other girls came up to speak, followed almost immediately by the harassed-looking little Mademoiselle.

"You are Dorothy Grayling, is it not?"

Dorothy had been accustomed to speaking French with her mother during many of those long hours on her sofa: it was to her quite a natural and instinctive thing to answer in that language— but she wished the next minute that she had not done so. True, Mademoiselle, with an immediate incredulous lighting up of her haggard little face, was instantly pouring out a reply of immense length and volubility; but all the girls within hearing seemed half-stunned with amazement. They fell back and stared, and Dorothy heard on all sides an astounded murmur.

"She can talk French! She's talking French *when she hasn't got to!*"

CHAPTER VI

"What Does F.G. Mean?"

THE journey from the Junction was very short, and for the whole of it Dorothy was monopolised by Mademoiselle. It must, of course (when your life is spent in teaching your own language to people who don't want to learn it), be an amazing comfort to meet with someone who speaks it easily and readily, and can understand every word you say. The girls in the same carriage stared with round eyes of amazement. Dorothy had evidently made a vast impression; but she was uneasily doubtful whether it was the sort of impression that she had wanted to make. However, poor little Mademoiselle did seem to be enjoying herself immensely, and that was really more important.

And then came the little country station, and large motor-buses that had been sent to meet the train. And then there was the meeting with Miss Chilcott; and Dorothy liked Miss Chilcott at sight, and Miss Chilcott appeared to like her. (But she was shrewd enough to understand at once what her mother had said about backing up a rather weak person, and shrewd enough, too, to feel glad of the appearance of Miss Pember—brusque and sharp-tongued and reliable, and obviously very fond indeed of Miss Chilcott.) And then Dorothy was in her cubicle, unpacking; a little relieved, perhaps, to find that Blanche was not one of the two other girls who shared the same room. One of these, it appeared, was still at home recovering from measles, and the other was a harmless cheerful soul named Caroline Cardigan, who was ready and willing to chatter about everything—Dorothy's awe-inspiring knowledge of French, the usual piggishness of Mademoiselle ("but she'll be decent to _you_, of course: she hates me, because I never can remember my Irregular Verbs"), the hatefulness of the Oxfords. She also mentioned that Miss Chilcott was "a dear; but you mustn't worry her about things, because it upsets her so—and we all hate her to be upset," and that

Miss Pember could be a perfect beast when she liked, but she was jolly just. Then about hockey and net-ball—

"You aren't allowed to play games? Oh, what a beastly shame!"

"I had to lie flat for a year and a half," Dorothy explained.

"I *say!*"

Caroline regarded her with horror.

"But I can walk and all that sort of thing quite well now," Dorothy hastened to explain. "Only I've got to wait till they're quite sure it's all right again before I may dance or drill or play games."

"Won't you be able to play tennis in the summer?"

"Oh, *I hope* so!" said Dorothy, with all her heart.

She had to explain, of course, how her accident had happened, and Caroline was duly impressed with her achievements in the Sports beforehand. And from that it was only a short step to her previous position in school games, and Caroline was impressed again.

"You must have been jolly good! How old were you?"

"Fourteen."

"Then you're sixteen now? Good! So am I."

It was a pleasing discovery, and they felt friendly at once: Caroline was, in fact, the sort of girl who makes friends readily with anyone. She went on good-naturedly to explain that Dorothy would miss comparatively little in not playing games this term.

"Most of the important matches come off before Christmas. We always get in as many as possible then, because *this* is the term when there's sure to be measles or something. But it's not so dull as you might expect, because we have the School Play at Easter, and there's a frightful lot of rehearsing and so on to be done for that. Can you act?"

Dorothy didn't know. The High School had never had a School Play.

"I'm jolly bad. I never can remember my lines," said Caroline frankly, "so they always give me quite a small part. But some people are frightfully good."

"What is the Play going to be?" Dorothy inquired, with deep interest.

"I don't know. We're never told till the beginning of the term. I think Miss Chilcott hunts one up in the Christmas hols., and plans out who is to be what."

Caroline chattered on volubly about who could act and who couldn't, and how frightfully clever Miss Tuke was about making dresses—but she was a perfect lamb, anyway—and what fun the rehearsals were till one got tired of them, and how horribly difficult it was to find a suitable part for Pills.

"Pills?" Dorothy repeated inquiringly.

"Phyllis Wills is her real name; but we always call her Pills," Caroline explained. "Her father's a doctor, you see. She's the Captain of the School, and so, of course, she must have a decent part; but she can't act for nuts, and she looks like nothing on earth!"

Dorothy was surprised at this free comment on such a dignitary; but it didn't seem her business to say so, and Caroline was chattering on.

"It was *very* different when Anita was Captain!"

"Who was Anita?"

"Come here—I'll show you!"

Caroline caught Dorothy by the arm and pulled her out of the room. Outside in the passage there were many photographs of school groups hanging framed on the walls, and before one of these Caroline stopped and pointed.

"That's Anita!" she said in a careful whisper, looking right and left to see that she was not overheard.

Dorothy looked with interest at the central figure of the group: a girl with a clever face and very pronounced features, and an immense fluff of hair standing out all round her head.

"What black hair! and what a lot of it!" she said.

"It wasn't black. It was bright red—but that always photographs black, you know," said Caroline.

"She's like somebody I know—I can't think who," said Dorothy, meditating in a puzzled way.

"Anita was like nobody but herself," said Caroline positively, leading the way back to her room. She shut the door with care before adding:

"*She was expelled!*"

"Expelled! How awful! What for?" cried Dorothy, quite suitably impressed.

"Oh, she *was* pretty awful! I'd only just come then, so I didn't know much about it; but she simply didn't care a hang for anybody, and she did exactly what she liked and cheeked everyone. She was so frightfully clever and did everything so well that people stood it much longer than they would have from anyone else; but at last she went a bit too far—I don't know exactly what it was that she did— and Miss Chilcott expelled her."

"How *awful!*" Dorothy repeated.

"Yes. I suppose it couldn't be helped—she was awful, as I said. But it did seem a pity. You can't think how she made everything go, especially the Play! It's been nothing like the same since. She could learn anything in no time, and she *could* act! It was just like seeing a proper actress on the stage. And she bucked up everyone else somehow, and made them do their best, and it all went like one o'clock! She even made Pills a little less like a stick; and the person who could do that could do *anything.*"

Dorothy felt a little sorry for Pills.

"I do trust some of the new girls can act, or we shall be pretty badly off," Caroline continued anxiously. "There's only one now who can remember her part *and* act it—Ada Ling, who has the cub. next to yours; and I believe—I'm not sure, of course—that *she* is an F.G."

Dorothy started.

"An F.G.?" she repeated.

"It's a Secret Society. *I've* never been asked to join it," said Caroline, in an unnaturally careless voice, "so I can't tell you much about it. It's *so* secret that outside people don't even know exactly who belongs, so you have to be jolly careful what you say, because you may be talking to an F.G. without knowing it!"

"What is it *for?*" Dorothy inquired, hoping that her voice did not betray her.

"Oh, *I* don't know, I'm sure! Some rot or other, I suppose," said Caroline.

"And what does F.G. mean?"

"I don't know—nobody knows. Some people say that they don't

know themselves!" said Caroline. "I say, there's the tea-bell and I haven't anything like unpacked."

She conducted Dorothy downstairs very kindly and sat by her, and continued her flow of information while she ate; but it had now, of course, to be in guarded language. Yes, *that* was the Captain of the School; and Dorothy gazed with interest at a small thin girl with spectacles, drinking tea in an absent-minded manner and hardly speaking to anyone. And the mistress at the end was Miss Tuke: the one with the—er—light hair. And that was Miss Adair, the games-mistress, and the one behind—but Dorothy had better not turn round—was Miss Scargill, who taught mathematics. After tea Miss Chilcott would have all the new girls in the drawing-room and talk to them; and supper was at eight, and lights were out at ten, and of course after that there was no speaking allowed. There weren't a frightful lot of rules, Dorothy would soon know them. And this was *real* raspberry jam—what luck! Later in the term it was generally supposed that fag-ends of different pots were mixed together and put on the table, and the result was not good. But the food was, on the whole, pretty decent—for a school. You weren't allowed butter with your marmalade; but there was quite good cake on Sundays.

Miss Scargill rose from the table—everyone else rising with her—and said: "Will all the new girls please go to Miss Chilcott in the drawing-room?" And then everyone dispersed.

Dorothy was hesitating a little, not quite sure of the way to the drawing-room; but this really seemed a very kind place, where everyone tried to make things easy for a newcomer.

"You don't know the way? I'll show you," said the black-eyed Rita Salmon, detaching herself from an august knot of Sixth Form people and mistresses; and Dorothy thanked her gratefully.

It seemed rather a long way: along a passage, and through a baize door that shut off the private side from the school. With her hand on this door, Rita paused.

"Don't forget to come to my room when you go to bed," she said, in her slow, heavy voice. "It's just opposite yours—number thirteen."

She pushed open the door, said: "That's the drawing-room, the door on the right," and vanished before Dorothy could answer.

There were only three other new girls, all quite small; and Miss Chilcott dismissed them after a very brief little talk. But she kept Dorothy with her for quite a long time, talking about her mother and their old school-days together, and all sorts of things, in the most delightful manner; it was quite easy to understand why Mrs. Grayling had said that girls always took to her.

"I am so glad to have you here, Dorothy," she ended. "And I hope you will be happy at St. Madern's."

"I am *sure* I shall, thank you, Miss Chilcott!" said Dorothy, with all her heart, and she went away feeling cheerful.

It was a little difficult to shake down at first in the big room where all the other girls were assembled; all so much at home, and knowing each other so well, and chattering away at such a rate. Dorothy could have occupied herself with the three small new girls, one of whom had been bathed in tears of home-sickness ever since her arrival; but Rita Salmon had already taken that office upon herself, and was amusing them very kindly in a corner with books out of the big library cupboard. Yes, St. Madern's *was* a kind place! Dorothy went a little shyly towards that big cupboard of books, which had attracted her book-loving eye from the very first; but she was not allowed to stand there isolated very long. First one girl and then another came over to speak to her, to ask what sort of books she liked, to discuss favourite authors; and in a very short time Dorothy was chattering away like the rest, and thoroughly enjoying herself. And then a loud bell rang suddenly, and everyone went hastily and got out pens and writing-blocks, and set to work letter-writing with great earnestness.

"We all send just a note home to-night, to say that we have arrived safely and all that," Dorothy's next neighbour explained to her. "The post goes at seven, so there's not time for much."

There was time for Dorothy, who was a quick writer, to say quite a good deal; and it was all in the most cheerful vein. She liked St. Madern's: she liked Miss Chilcott very much: she had a jolly girl in the next cubicle to her own: she was sure that she was going to be ever so happy. Only of the F.G. she said nothing, because she felt so extremely vague about it that there was really nothing to say—till next time.

"And I *do* hope you are not too lonely, darling; and won't the holidays be lovely!" she ended hastily; for the bell was ringing again, and there was hurried blotting and smudging in all directions, and a rustle of folding paper, and wails for stamps from one improvident person and another.

"Come along and finish unpacking; and we've got to change for supper," said Caroline Cardigan in her ear, thumping down a well-licked envelope with great vigour.

Dorothy had finished her unpacking; but she went readily to lend a hand to the rather untidy Caroline, whose possessions lay strewn in all directions about her cubicle; and there was comparing of photographs and pictures, and discussing of homes and relations, and a general friendly getting to know one another. It seemed a very short time to both before the loud bell rang again for supper, and after that there was a pleasant hour in the drawing-room with Miss Chilcott, and then a weeding-out of the little ones for bed, and finally at quarter past nine, which was bedtime for even the Sixth Form.

Dorothy had been wondering a little uncomfortably how she was to shake herself free of the friendly Caroline in order to obey her summons to Number Thirteen. But this difficulty smoothed itself away, as difficulties are apt to do if one doesn't worry over them; for Caroline was kept back by Miss Chilcott for some last word of direction, and it was quite easy for Dorothy to slip away alone. She ran up the stairs with a crowd of other girls; but they all turned off in other directions, and she finally found herself alone at her own door, looking rather timidly at a large "13" on the door opposite. The unknown is always a little alarming; and Dorothy felt very much of a new girl, as she knocked modestly and heard herself bidden to come in.

It was a small room: much smaller, of course, than the one which herself shared with two others. Rita seemed to be a person of orderly habits, for everything was unpacked and stowed away, and there was not so much as a pin out of place. There were things about it of a dignified nature, fitting for a member of Sixth Form: a bright scarlet wadded quilt on the bed (Dorothy had only brought a thick travelling rug), and brushes with tortoiseshell backs, and some expensive-looking pictures on the walls.

"Well? What is it?" Rita asked her, most unexpectedly.

She had an immensely thick pigtail of black hair, and she was unplaiting this, and watching Dorothy in the glass as she spoke, without turning round.

"You—you told me to come," Dorothy stammered, in great confusion.

"*Did* I? Why?"

If Dorothy had been confused before, she was doubly so now. Had she made some awful mistake? *Wasn't* there any Secret Society, after all? *Hadn't* Rita said, only just after tea: "Come to my room at bedtime?"

"The—the F.G.—"

Dorothy paused, scarlet and abashed.

"Dear me! and what do you know about the F.G.?"

Rita's cool, slow voice had no expression in it of any sort; but she was smiling a little in the glass.

"Nothing at all. But you told me—"

"You know, of course, that it's against the rules to go to another girl's room?"

"I—I quite forgot," said Dorothy, in a sorely troubled voice. (Yes, that *had* been one of the things that Miss Chilcott had mentioned in her after-tea talk. But—surely—a Sixth Form girl wouldn't *invite* a new girl to break rules?)

"Let me see—what is your name?"

Poor Dorothy gave it, in a shaking voice that was barely audible. (This was surely the last humiliation of all, that Rita shouldn't even remember who she was!)

"Dorothy Grayling: oh, yes!" said the slow, cool voice. "Yes. It's all right. I did invite you to join the F.G., didn't I—when we were waiting at the Junction?"

"Yes, you did," Dorothy murmured faintly, with a very small hope rising at the bottom of her heart.

Rita finished brushing and replaiting her hair: she tied it with a red-ribbon bow and turned round.

"It's all right," she said again, in quite a different voice, and her smile was really wonderfully attractive. "Yes. I think you are quite suitable for the F.G. It's a very *Secret* Society, you know. We don't talk about it to outsiders."

"Oh, no!" Dorothy hastened to agree eagerly.

"Well—I don't know that there is very much to explain to you. The pass-word is *Jonah*. It isn't easy to have a General Meeting very often; but I hope to have one, at least, this term. The ordinary meetings—let me see."

Rita considered for a minute or two.

"They're announced on the Notice Board, but of course one has to say as little as possible, so you must remember for yourself. When you see the announcement on the board, you go to the cloak-room passage, just outside the cloak-room door, on Tuesday directly after tea—you won't forget?"

"Oh, no!" Dorothy promised effusively: though in her heart of hearts she thought this a curiously public place for the meeting of a Secret Society.

Rita took a bunch of keys out of her pocket and proceeded to unlock a drawer, then a desk that was inside it, then a little leather box that was inside the desk, and finally a small book that had a lock and key of its own. In this book she made a brief and careful note, and then she locked up everything again in reverse order. It was very impressive and secret.

"Well—I think that is all for now. Good night."

Dorothy hesitated.

"You aren't worrying about having broken a rule? Well, don't! They're all rather elastic the first evening, and anyhow, of course I wouldn't report you. The F.G. stand by each other *always*," said Rita.

"Yes—thank you, Rita. But it—it wasn't that," said Dorothy.

"What, then?"

"Please—what does F.G. mean?"

The question sounded awfully bold when it was spoken and yet—*wasn't* it a reasonable thing to ask? Dorothy had been quite sure of that; and yet, as Rita stood silent, the sureness suddenly faded. After all, she was only a new girl, and Rita was in the Sixth. Had she given offence by a piece of impertinent curiosity? How awful!

Rita opened her door, and looked out casually, up and down the passage.

"All clear—no one will see you, if you're quick," she said. And presumably she was not angry, for she once more gave that unexpected attractive smile.

"Good night, Jonah!" she said.

IT took a surprisingly short time to make Dorothy feel quite at home at St. Madern's: yes, even though she had to give up various things that other girls did, and to do various things from which they were free. It *was* very hard at first to see them going gaily off to hockey and net-ball, while she stayed behind to lie flat on her back; and the daily massage was tedious and rather painful. But then, as she bravely reminded herself, what a glorious improvement her present life was on what it had been a year ago! And the school doctor was most encouraging when he made his weekly examination, and Miss Adair was a dear, telling stories and making jokes while she massaged, and the weary lying flat was done in the drawing-room in peace and quiet, with any amount of books to beguile the time, and Miss Chilcott's gramophone, and sometimes Miss Chilcott herself to talk in her delightful way. Besides—one tremendous advantage—

"I don't think I should have given you such a long part in the play, Dorothy, if I hadn't known that you would have plenty of spare time for learning it."

The play proved to be *A Midsummer Night's Dream*, and Dorothy scored immensely from the beginning by having once done it for an exam. at the High School. There was a most thrilling moment, on the first day of term, when Miss Chilcott finished reading other notices at the end of prayers, and then announced what she had chosen and read out a list of the performers. The whole school listened breathlessly, each waiting for her own name. As Miss Chilcott walked out of the hall afterwards, with the other mistresses following her, an instant buzz broke out like the noise of a hive of bees.

"Well, I do think I might have had one of the decent parts with jolly Greek clothes!" Quince protested bitterly.

"I shall never have time to get through all Bottom's part!" Kitty

Halliday shrieked. "Yes, I've seen the play and I know how much there is!—though it's rather a jolly part of course, with the ass's head and all."

"Celia will do awfully well for Titania, and Gwen Rivers will *look* rather nice as Oberon—if she ever remembers what she has to say!"

"I suppose Theseus isn't much of a part, or they wouldn't have given it to Pills!"

If the girls had but known it, an almost equally animated (though less noisy) discussion was going on amongst the mistresses at the same moment.

"Yes, Miss Pember," Miss Chilcott defended herself, "I know quite well that Phyllis won't look in the least like a Duke of Athens; but it's such a dull part that she can't do much harm with it. Of course it's a pity that Caroline is so much taller, but you *can't* have a short Queen of the Amazons."

"Bottom seems rather a large part for Kitty," Miss Pember suggested drily.

"It's a *noisy* part, and she can shriek and rant as much as she likes—and she'll do that in any case, as we know by past experience."

"Isn't it rather unusual to give a perfectly new girl such a prominent part as Helena?"

"Helena must be tall and fair," said Miss Chilcott, "and—perhaps I wouldn't have done it in every case. But Dorothy is so handicapped, poor child, that I give her a very long part on purpose, to make up a little for all those weary hours of lying flat. Besides, I think she's a clever girl, and she *looks* as if she could act—though you never know, of course, till you actually begin to rehearse."

"Rita is exactly my idea of Hermia," Miss Adair remarked briskly.

"Yes. I think she should be good—if she can get up a little animation in the quarrelling scene," Miss Chilcott agreed "Ada Ling is a little too big for Puck, I'm afraid, but she acts so extremely well that I really couldn't give the part to anyone else."

"What they'll all *want*, of course," said Miss Pember shrewdly, "is to take the parts with attractive clothes. I don't suppose there are two girls in the school who would have sense enough to choose Bottom rather than Hippolyta!"

"You are always very severe, Miss Pember," said Miss Chilcott, laughing a little. "I'm sure I know two, at least!"

Miss Pember looked at her with her little sharp, dark eyes.

"We are thinking of the same two, I'm sure, Miss Chilcott," she said, "and—I'm not too sure about one of them!"

The rehearsals began almost at once; and the first of them was so appallingly unsuccessful that Dorothy—who was unused to any sort of theatricals—felt positive that nothing could ever be made of anybody and said so, though only in the strictest privacy to Caroline in the seclusion of their bedroom.

"Oh, it will work out all right—you'll see!" said that young lady optimistically. "It's *always* like nothing on earth to begin with. But Miss Pember is a frightfully good coach."

"It's a good thing we began at once," said Dorothy, still secretly of her own opinion.

"We always begin at once, before anyone has time to start measles or anything," said Caroline philosophically. "*That* is what makes things really difficult. I don't think Miss Chilcott knows a minute's peace till the first three weeks or so are over. It's pretty safe after that, of course, because we sit right at the back in church and there aren't any shops for us to go to—and this term there isn't any half-term holiday, just for that reason. It does seem rather hard, but I daresay it's quite a good thing, considering—and we get two days tacked on to the Easter holidays instead."

"Nobody seems to have *any* idea of acting," said Dorothy, reverting to her first anxieties.

"You can't act while you're only reading your part," Caroline assured her. "Nobody could. Some of them are awful sticks anyhow, of course—Pills can't act for nuts and never could and never will. But you wait till Ada comes back next Monday! *She* can act all right; and it's wonderful how one decent actor will wake up all the others."

And, much to Dorothy's surprise, this proved to be the case. Ada Ling was a quiet, unremarkable person, rather short, with a very turned-up nose, but you forgot all that from the very first lines of her opening speech—she was Puck and nobody else. She had learnt a great deal of her part during the seclusion of quarantine, Miss Chilcott having thoughtfully written and told her what it was to be, and that of course was a tremendous asset. She woke up the rather heavy and wooden Oberon into something like life; and this in turn affected Titania, the languid and delicate Celia Tanner, and made her speak up and put some energy into her part. It began to occur to several people, for the first time in their lives, that the play—even though it *was* Shakespeare—was not only interesting, but funny. With the first spontaneous laugh from a looker-on, Miss Pember's anxious brow relaxed for the first time. The rehearsal closed on quite a cheerful note, and even Dorothy began dimly to see that things might shape themselves with patience.

"And we're nearly over the three weeks!" said Caroline comfortably, in their room that night. "I don't think anyone *can* start anything now. Ada, are you *quite* sure that you were properly disinfected and haven't brought any measle-germs back with you?"

"I'm *quite* sure!" Ada replied, with feeling. "Why, all my things simply reek still—can't you smell them? I put my nose into my bedroom while the formalin lamp was burning and I only just got out in time—it was too awful for words!"

"Is there anything Pills hasn't had? She's generally the first to start anything!" said Caroline.

"Or else one of the little new kids," Ada agreed. "There are three of them this term."

"I'll ask them what they've had already," said Caroline, who was something of a fusser.

She carried out this laudable plan next day, catching the three little new girls all with their heads together over the same book; and the result was most satisfactory. All of them had had measles and chicken-pox and whooping-cough, and one of them even proudly announced that she had had scarlet fever. Caroline commended them all very highly.

"What is the joke?" Rita inquired, coming up with a magazine.

"Only we're so jolly near the limit of anybody's developing anything infectious, and these three good infants have had everything already," Caroline explained briskly. "Measles and whooping-cough and chicken-pox, and Dora's even had scarlet fever—excellent kid!"

Rita only smiled—she was a person of few words—and sat

down in the chair over which Caroline was leaning; but it was quite obvious that the latter was not wanted, and she accordingly melted away with some speed. You never, somehow, got a chance to forget that Rita was in the Sixth, as you might with Kitty or Gwen or even Celia. She wasn't a person with whom you took liberties, though she wasn't pretty, or brilliantly clever, or very prominent in any way. Even with her own contemporaries she was not particularly popular; but no one could deny that she was extraordinarily nice to the little ones. Caroline, looking back from the door, saw the three little heads all as close as they could get to the black one with the long pigtail.

The excitement of the play had distracted all thoughts from anything (out of school hours) unconnected with it. When Dorothy came down the next morning and found a small crowd round the Notice Board in the hall, her first thought was that it was some announcement of a change in the time of rehearsal, or that some alteration had been made in the cast; and she hoped, with a little jump of alarm, that *Helena* was not going to be taken away from her, when she had already learnt so many of her lines and was beginning to get some idea of the character. Of course, she had never acted before, and it *was* a big part to give to a new girl—she was quite well aware that there had been jealous looks and words of surprise, when Miss Chilcott first read out her list of characters. But she had done her very best with it, and last time Miss Pember—never too ready with praise—had actually commended her.

She was one of the tallest girls in the school—thanks to those long months of lying on a sofa—and she could read easily over the shoulders of most of the others. There was only one new notice on the Board: a very small one in a corner, not typed as usual, but printed in block-letters.

"THE F.G. WILL MEET AS USUAL THIS WEEK."

There was a murmur all about the Board; and Dorothy stood back, quickly hoping that no one would see how red she had turned. In the greater excitement of the play, she had forgotten all about the F.G., had almost ceased to believe in its existence. She wondered for how many of the little crowd that notice meant anything; but it was impossible to tell. Everyone was staring, and there were so many exclamations of: "There it is again!" "I wonder what it really means?" "What *is* the F.G.—doesn't *anyone* know?"—that, if some people in the group were silent, it was next to impossible to identify them. If you thought that one girl looked flushed and queer, the next moment you heard her exclaiming with the others, and so knew that it was only your own guilty fancy. And there wasn't long to wait, in any case. This was Monday. On Tuesday after tea, outside the cloak-room door, Dorothy would find out for certain who were her fellow-members.

She learnt very little of her part on either of those two days. Try as she would, lying flat on her back in the drawing-room, to fasten her attention on Helena quarrelling with Hermia, it would wander to the passage outside the cloak-room. The rehearsals seemed dull and she was glad to get them over, and lessons had lost a good deal of their interest—but Monday always was the day that she most disliked, for it contained both geometry and botany. On Tuesday at tea-time she had next to no appetite; and, noting this curious fact, she looked up and down the long table in an eager attempt to discover if anyone else was similarly affected. But no. Tea and bread and butter and marmalade and jam all seemed to be disappearing in the usual business-like manner. Possibly, therefore, Dorothy was the *only* new member this term. The F.G. might be most strictly limited in number, and she had been chosen to fill some gap left by a girl who had just left. It was a flattering thought.

Chairs were pushed back on the polished floor with the usual clatter and the usual buzz of conversation accompanied the usual forming of little groups, as everyone went out of the tea-room; for there was a lucid interval now for half an hour, before Preparation began at a quarter to six. Dorothy shook off one or two girls who showed signs of being companionable, and slipped off by herself. Her heart was beating rather fast.

In the long passage that led to the cloakroom there was no one at all.

Well—she *had* come away as fast as possible and hurried, in her fear of being late. Other people perhaps had not been able to escape from their friends so easily. But it was rather an embarrassingly public place to wait, with no reason to give if any mistress caught her there. She went into the cloak-room and hunted in her coat pocket for a handkerchief that wasn't there, and that took a minute or two; but when she came back the passage was still empty. Dorothy felt herself growing hot about the ears and cold about the hands. Had she mistaken the day?—but no, she could hear Rita's slow voice saying: "Tuesday after tea." And, for the same reason, she knew that she was right in the meeting-place. What could be wrong, then? And was it easier to stand facing down the passage so that she would see everyone who came, or pretend to be interested in something in the cloak-room? She tried both, and found them equally embarrassing; and nothing happened. Finally, as a last resource, she untied her shoe laces—both of them—and knelt down to tie them up again very carefully and slowly, giving her whole attention to the business. *Was* someone coming at last? But she had fancied that so many times already, and turned round to find herself mistaken. She would not look up until she had done both laces with all possible elaboration.

"Good evening, Jonah!"

Dorothy was on her feet again with one movement, very red—much redder than any amount of stooping would account for. She couldn't be mistaken in that voice! And she wasn't. It was Rita: only Rita, looking faintly amused.

"How splendid to be so punctual! I see you are going to be an excellent F.G."

There didn't seem anything to say to that, and it was impossible to turn any redder. Dorothy only looked—she couldn't help it— down the empty passage.

"No," said Rita, interpreting that glance, which, indeed, was easy enough. "You needn't do that. There is no one else coming."

"No one else!" Dorothy repeated in astonishment.

Again Rita read her thoughts with the utmost ease.

"The F.G. doesn't consist of only you and me—don't begin to think that!" she said, with the faintly amused look deepening into a laugh. "But it really *is* a very Secret Society, you see, and so people don't always meet at the same time—except at General Meetings, of course. I hope we shall have one of those this term, but not yet."

"Oh!" said Dorothy feebly.—But the Notice Board had said:

"The F.G. will meet as usual this week"! She was so deeply puzzled, that she stammered out something to this effect.

"Yes, certainly," Rita agreed. "But everyone is given her own time and place of meeting, of course, and keeps to it."

She gazed amiably at Dorothy, watching this piece of information sink in. Well—it was quite easy to understand, when one had once grasped it; and perhaps the best way, Dorothy could quite see, to keep a Secret Society really secret.

"Your time and place will always be the same—as far as I can tell now," Rita informed her. "And there is only one thing for you to do this time: a very small thing."

"Yes?" Dorothy responded eagerly.

Rita drew a paper from her pocket: just a torn piece of letter paper, with writing on one side.

"You are to run upstairs—now, as fast as you can—and drop this over the bannisters into the hall," she said.

"And—drop—?" Dorothy repeated in amazement.

"You heard what I said!" Rita answered, with a sudden sharpness. "Now—quick! I needn't tell *you* not to read it, of course. That's probably why you were chosen for the job, instead of—some of the others."

With this implied compliment to encourage her, Dorothy ran like the wind on her foolish errand—the most foolish errand, surely, that any member of a Secret Society had ever been asked to perform! She flew up the stairs, round to the landing where there was a sort of well, looking down into the hall; and from that standpoint she let her absurd piece of paper flutter downwards from her hand—just in time, as it proved. For a moment later, as she still looked down, Miss Chilcott came walking slowly into the hall, talking to Rita as she came. Dorothy was sincerely glad that she had not had to do her job now, when the paper would probably have landed on the head of the Head Mistress. She was sincerely glad, in any case, to have finished such an idiotic piece of business, and now she could go downstairs again and settle down to preparation as usual—practically no wiser than she had been at first about the mysterious F.G.

"Yes, Rita. I think you are quite right about the dresses—but there is plenty of time to settle that, and I am rather in a hurry now," said Miss Chilcott; and she nodded and went on, while Rita modestly vanished towards the preparation room.

There are people who will walk over or round some little thing dropped on the floor a dozen times rather than pick it up, because it is not their business to sweep and tidy, and there are people who cannot bear to see anything out of place. Miss Chilcott belonged to the latter class. She stooped and picked up the piece of torn paper. ...

It was a minute or two later that Miss Pember came into the hall in her brisk fashion, and stopped short with an exclamation.

"Miss Chilcott—what *is* the matter?"

Miss Chilcott was sitting on a hall-chair, and her face was white. She looked up as Miss Pember came quickly towards her.

"*This* is the matter," she said, in a faint voice. She held up the torn piece of paper, and Miss Pember took it and read it.

"Well? What about it?" she asked sharply.

"Don't you *see?* It's from Anita—Anita Lyon. Someone in the school is still corresponding with her!"

Miss Pember read it again—the very little that there was of it.

"You remember what she said when she left?" Miss Chilcott asked, in a queer strained voice.

Miss Pember nodded crisply.

"She means it still—she's *writing* it still, to someone who is here now!"

"You can't be sure it's from Anita," said Miss Pember.

"I *am* sure."

"It might just as well be—Rita, for instance!"

"It isn't in the least like Rita's writing."

"It isn't like anybody's writing, for that matter," said Miss Pember. "It's a sort of printing—not even script."

"Who but Anita would want to write like that—so that no one should guess the sender of the letter?"

"My dear," said Miss Pember—she had known Miss Chilcott for a great many years and she was considerably the elder of the two—"you really are perfectly foolish about that Anita girl! You've let her get on your nerves, and it's a pity. How long is it since she left—two years? Well, we've never heard anything of her from that day to this—and I really do think it is absurd to set her up as a bogey after all this time! She has probably forgotten the existence of all of us, long ago."

Miss Chilcott pointed, with a little shiver, to the third line on the torn paper.

"Absurd! absurd!" said Miss Pember. "It's the most unlikely thing in the world. Do try to put it out of your mind altogether—or make up your mind, as I said, that the thing is Rita's."

"It can't be Rita's. She was talking to me here just now—she'd been to the cloak-room to get a handkerchief, and she wanted to ask something about dresses for the play. She hasn't been through here at all."

"Well, I should like to ask her, just for my own satisfaction," said Miss Pember. She called sharply to someone passing in the distance:

"Ada! Just tell Rita to come here for a minute!"

"Yes, Miss Pember!" answered a distant voice; and after a very brief pause—during which Miss Chilcott shivered and Miss Pember stood frowning at the paper in her hand—Rita came, quite cool, and calm, and collected.

"Yes, Miss Pember? Ada said you wanted me."

"Is this yours?" Miss Pember asked abruptly, putting the paper into her hand.

"This? What is it?"

Rita turned it about with an admirable surprise and bewilderment.

"Read it!" Miss Pember directed briefly.

"But—there's almost nothing to read!" said Rita, obeying.

"Now—did you write that?"

"*I?* Oh, *no*, Miss Pember! Why, it isn't my writing!"

"That is not always a conclusive argument," said Miss Pember drily. "Do you know anything about it?"

"No! I never saw it before. What does it mean!" asked Rita, raising black eyes of perfect innocence.

"Nothing, I should imagine. But I thought you might like to have it back, if it *was* yours," said Miss Pember drily. "That's all. Thank you!"

"*Now*, do you believe me?" asked Miss Chilcott, when Rita had taken a deferential departure and they were alone again.

"Since we are such old friends—and since no one belonging to the school is within hearing," said Miss Pember, "I'll tell you what I do think. I think you are a perfect goose, and I hope I shall never hear Anita Lyon's name again as long as I live!"

CHAPTER VIII

A Fright and a Wetting

"DOROTHY must get pretty sick of lying down like that every day—even though it *is* in the drawing-room!" said a compassionate person, going off to hockey.

"Well, it gives her loads of time to do prep., of course, and learn that huge part she's got in the play," said somebody else, more critical and less sympathetic. "Besides, she has the gramophone when she likes, and Miss Chilcott is often and often in there talking to her. I think she has rather a good time, if you ask me."

"Besides, she writes stories," said Caroline Cardigan. "Didn't you know? Oh, yes, stories out of her own head. She won't let anyone see them and I only found out by accident. But I expect they're jolly good. She tells us the most *ripping* stories in bed at night, before ten. But she's frightfully conscientious, she won't go on for a single minute after that."

"What sort of stories?" several people wanted to know.

"Oh, all sorts! Funny ones and detectives and the usual kind," said Caroline. "She seems to have read the most frightful amount—books that I've never even heard of! I suppose it was when she had to lie flat for all that time, after her accident. She must have been bored!"

"I wish Caroline wouldn't make her tell so many detectives and that sort of thing," Ada Ling complained, swinging open the gate of the games field. "I hate frightening stories; and that one she told us last night was really *awful*. I couldn't go to sleep for ages, and when I did I dreamt about it."

"You idiot! It was perfectly ripping!" said Caroline. "I shall ask for something of the same sort to-night."

And she did, which was very flattering to Dorothy—a story-teller likes to feel that her efforts are appreciated. She ransacked her brain, and finally raked up a tale that she had heard years ago and half forgotten, called: "By One, by Two, and by Three." She furbished up her remembrances carefully, lying flat in the drawing-room, and added to them here and there, and finally produced a very creditable thriller, which, when the time came, was most effective. In fact, it proved *too* effective, for Ada screamed with terror halfway through and cried and begged her to leave off.

"Lunatic! It's splendid!" cried the stronger-nerved Caroline. "Go on, Dorothy!"

But Dorothy, a little alarmed, wouldn't. She liked horrors herself, but she was sufficiently sympathetic to understand that other people didn't. The big clock struck ten while they were still arguing the point, and put an automatic end to the dispute. But Ada walked in her sleep that night, very terrifyingly, and was only caught by Dorothy—who mercifully happened to be awake—just as she was opening the door and preparing to walk out in her nightgown.

The whole school knew next day, of course; it is wonderful how that sort of news flies through a crowd of girls with quite incredible swiftness. There were those who envied the room that afforded such thrills and said so, openly wishing that Dorothy could be transferred to their tamer quarters. There were those who sympathised with Ada and said so too, admonishing Dorothy in good set terms. There was one person who listened to all this in silence and then went softly away, knocking decorously at the door of Miss Chilcott's office, where she transacted state affairs and saw people on business.

"Come in! What is it, Rita?"

"Are you very busy, Miss Chilcott? Could I speak to you for a minute?"

"I am very busy, because I have been interrupted once already this morning," said Miss Chilcott not too warmly. "Can't you wait till after dinner?"

"I think you *ought* to know, Miss Chilcott."

"Very well, then. Only be as quick as you can."

Miss Chilcott put her watch on the table in a pointed manner, and leaned back in her chair.

"I am sorry to say that Ada Ling has been walking in her sleep again, Miss Chilcott."

"Yes? That is a pity, for I hoped she had outgrown that failing."

"Yes, I know," Rita agreed smoothly. "I remember how worried you were when she used to do it. That was why I thought you ought to know at once."

"Quite right," said Miss Chilcott.

"—and the cause of it," Rita went on unbrokenly. "I hate telling tales, Miss Chilcott—"

"A hateful custom," Miss Chilcott agreed immediately.

"But I think you *ought* to know that the real reason was some story that Dorothy Grayling told in bed at night. I don't know what it was—but it must have been something most unsuitable and frightening."

Rita paused modestly.

"You didn't think, I suppose," said Miss Chilcott rather drily, "of speaking to Dorothy first—it is the business of the Sixth Form, of course, to see that this sort of thing doesn't occur—and suggesting that *she* should come and confess for herself?"

"No, Miss Chilcott!" said Rita, looking up with large expressionless black eyes. "I thought you ought to know *at once*, and—and a girl who would do a thing like that would not be very likely to tell on herself, would she?"

There was another little pause.

"I am afraid, Rita," said Miss Chilcott, in a drier voice than ever, "that you are not a particularly good judge of character. Dorothy Grayling came to me the first thing after breakfast—without any urging from anybody—to confess and take all the blame on herself. She was in the most dreadful distress about it. I am not in the least afraid that the same thing will ever happen again. And it must please be remembered that she had never heard of Ada's tendency to sleep-walking, and had no reason to suppose that she would be unusually affected by a story that would only be pleasantly thrilling to girls with stronger nerves. Do you want to tell me anything else about anybody?"

"No, thank you, Miss Chilcott," said Rita decorously, and went out of the room with great quietness and propriety. She did not mention to anyone where she had been, or on what errand. Neither did she take any steps to check the people who were still vociferously saying that Dorothy ought to be ashamed of herself.

"I *am!*—but I didn't mean any harm," said poor Dorothy, defending herself with blazing cheeks.

"Not meaning isn't any good. You ought to have thought!" said her stern accusers. And a most unpleasant feeling prevailed for nearly all that day—till, in fact, Miss Chilcott happened to overhear something of it and instantly intervened.

"Stop, girls! No one is to say that sort of thing again," she said. "Dorothy made a mistake—as we all do sometimes—without in the least intending it, and she came to confess *instantly* to me, as soon as she realised what she had done. I am sure she will be the last person in the school to make that sort of mistake again. I wish everyone was as ready to confess her fault, when things go wrong!"

She said the last words pointedly, before she went away. And—though she had looked at no one in particular, except the scarlet Dorothy—everyone recognised the allusion to Hester Tyke, who had broken a bedroom jug several days ago, and let the blame rest upon a little new servant. There were no more remarks about Ada's unfortunate habit of sleep-walking; and Dorothy soon found that the affair had blown over and that she was no longer regarded as a pariah among her fellows.

It was an extraordinarily wet day, too wet to give any hopes of going out at all; and this is always trying. The rehearsal went languidly, because everybody needed fresh air and couldn't get it. Mademoiselle's temper seemed even less reliable than ever. There was dancing in the afternoon, as walking was impossible; but the day was stuffy as well as wet and people soon got too hot and left off. Tea-time seemed a long way off, and the miserable grey day closed in very early. It was nearly dark when Kitty, standing dismally by a window, suddenly exclaimed at the top of her voice, after her fashion:

"Who *on earth* is this?"

Several other people, joining her languidly, stared at a small dripping figure which had crept out from under the shelter of some bushes lining the drive, and was making a hurried run toward the side door.

"Who is it?"

"Who *can* it be, on such a day?"

"Why—it's Blanche Bates!"

"Blanche Bates! It *can't* be!"

"But it *is*," said the last speaker positively; and she was right.

A stream of incredulous girls ran from the big hall, where they had been dancing, to the side door; and there, wet and shivering, stood the incredible Blanche. She was evidently scared out of her life.

"*Where* have you been, Blanche Bates?" cried Kitty.

"N—n—nowhere," gasped the dripping one, in a very faint voice.

"Nowhere? Then how did you get in that state, pray?" demanded Kitty, the only Sixth Form girl present, as it happened, and so full of authority.

"It—it's raining," Blanche faltered wildly.

"Yes, we're all quite well aware of that, thank you. Where have you *been* in the rain?"

Blanche turned scared eyes from one face to another, as if looking for something that she did not find. She shivered and shivered.

"You'd better come to Miss Chilcott at once," ordered Kitty.

"Hadn't she better go and change first? She's rather delicate, and she's simply soaking," Dorothy suggested. Her heart smote her a little at sight of that forlorn little figure; for she *had* meant to be very good to Blanche, knowing her at home, and as a matter of fact she had seen scarcely anything of her. "I'll take her upstairs, and you go and tell Miss Chilcott, Kitty."

It was rather cheek, of course, from a person only in the Fifth; but it was really sound sense, and Blanche was most cold and forlorn, and Kitty was kind-hearted. She said therefore, after a moment's hesitation: "All right—take her up quick!" and ran off to the drawing-room.

Dorothy ran her charge upstairs in double-quick time; for she remembered alarmedly how often Mrs. Bates had talked of Blanche's delicacy, and what care she needed, and how she mustn't be allowed to have a cold on her chest under any circumstances. Such a cold seemed at this moment the likeliest thing in the world; and Dorothy stripped and briskly rubbed and hastily clothed again the shivering Blanche without wasting any time in unnecessary questions. She was so speedy, indeed, that she had very nearly finished her job before Miss Chilcott came in, and that was soon enough.

"Oh, that's right, Dorothy! How splendidly quick you have been!"

Blanche had stopped shivering, feeling the comfort of dry and warm clothes, but she began again now—this time obviously with fright.

"Blanche, why *did* you go out in the rain?"

Blanche only shivered.

"Tell me!" said Miss Chilcott, kindly, but with authority.

"Nobody ever said—not to," Blanche murmured foolishly.

"Nobody ever thought of anyone's wanting to do such a thing, on such a day," said Miss Chilcott. "Where have you been?"

"Only—a little way down the drive—"

"Why?"

"I didn't—I didn't do anything naughty!" Blanche suddenly burst out, with tears and sobbing.

"But why did you want to go—"

"I—I didn't want—"

"Did anyone ask you to go?"

But that question seemed the last straw. Blanche's crying became a tempest, and her shivering was like an ague. It was obviously quite useless to go on questioning her and Miss Chilcott gave it up.

"You are hardly more than a baby, we all know; but you mustn't be a naughty baby, and you must learn to be sensible and not do silly things like this," she said, quite kindly. "I don't think you are fit to come downstairs again to-day, so you must go to bed and stay there, *like* a baby. Dorothy, I am sorry you have had the trouble of dressing her for nothing. Will you please see her into bed? and I will send up her tea and a hot-water bottle."

Dorothy was suddenly smitten with a pang of remorse. She was extremely anxious, after this morning's fiasco, never again to do anything at St. Madern's that she shouldn't.

"*I am* sorry! I quite forgot that we are not allowed to go into each other's rooms, when I brought Blanche up in such a hurry!" she said anxiously.

"There are exceptions to every rule, and I don't consider that you have broken this one, under the circumstances," Miss Chilcott smiled at her; and she went away.

The hot bottle came and the tea; and by the time the big tea-bell rang, Dorothy had her charge very snugly in bed, not crying any more, with her face washed and her hands getting warm. They had been like little bits of frozen raw meat.

"Now are you all right, Blanche?"

"Yes, Dorothy. Thank you, Dorothy."

"And you won't be a little goose and do silly things like that again?"

"No. I'm sorry," Blanche murmured meekly.

"Drink your tea while it's hot," Dorothy admonished her, setting the tray carefully on a chair close to the bed. It reminded her of those many, many teas and breakfasts and dinners that she herself had eaten off a tray, lying flat. "Now I must go."

"Dorothy!"

Blanche had suddenly pulled herself up in bed. Her little face looked pinched and anxious.

"Yes?" said Dorothy, turning at the door.

"Please—*please* will you bring me up my attaché-case?"

"You won't be expected to do any prep. to-night, I'm sure."

"No—but I want it. Oh, please, *please* let me have it!"

Blanche looked so very much like breaking out into tears again, that Dorothy nodded hastily and ran downstairs; it seemed the easiest way. She found the little absurd attaché-case, dear to the hearts of all the small girls in the school, among a pile of others and marked with its owner's initials in black letters; and ran up with it again. There was almost no one about, of course; but at the turn of the passage she met Rita.

"The tea-bell went minutes ago, Dorothy," she observed, in her slow voice.

"Yes, I know. I'll be down in one minute."

Dorothy ran on her way; but she felt uncomfortably that there was nothing about her that Rita's black eyes had not taken in in that brief interview—her hurry, and the attaché-case, and her being up on that landing where she had no business. She opened the door of Blanche's room with haste.

"Here you are, Blanche. I can't wait—I'm late already.—Why, what is the matter *now?*"

Blanche was cowering down in her bed as if she were frightened, and she had not touched her tea. She sobbed out: "N—nothing!" in a voice that shook deplorably.

"*Is* there anything the matter?" Dorothy asked again, with a little impatience.

But Blanche only shook her head dumbly, retreating still further under the bedclothes; and it was more than tea-time, and Dorothy might get into trouble for being so late. Besides, the child always had been a silly, spoilt little thing, and it was probably quite useless to waste time in trying to make her speak if she didn't mean to.

Dorothy shut the door after her, perhaps a little sharply, and went downstairs.

CHAPTER IX

Rita's Toothache

"IS Blanche all right this morning?" Dorothy inquired next morning of Hester Pyke, who slept in the same room.

"No. She was awfully sick in the night—little pig!" said Hester, in the justly-injured tone of one who has been deprived of her lawful sleep by someone else's fault.

"Well, she didn't get anything yesterday to *make* her sick. There was no cake or anything for tea," Dorothy argued, defending the absent.

"It's not the first time," said Hester gloomily; and went off to practice.

Miss Chilcott, as a matter of fact, was making the same comment to Miss Pember at the same time in other words.

"I can't understand why Blanche should get upset like this. I *did* think I had stopped all that sort of thing, when I made a rule of sweets only on Sundays and no home-parcels of food."

"Some children are naturally bilious," said Miss Pember. "Besides, she probably caught a severe chill out in the rain last night."

"Yes. I'm afraid that must be it," said Miss Chilcott. "I'd better take her temperature."

She went upstairs, reflecting that Anglo-Indian children, with their parents several weeks away, are something of an anxiety. And she took Blanche's temperature; and Blanche, in the ordinary phrase, hadn't got one. But she looked very white and peaked and miserable, and she hadn't been able to touch her breakfast.

"Well, Blanche, you must stay in bed to-day, and you must have the usual remedy," said Miss Chilcott. She knew that "the usual remedy" (which was castor-oil) was more dreaded by most people than any ordinary punishment. "No sweets next Sunday, of course; and you must eat nothing but dry toast to-day."

"Yes, Miss Chilcott," Blanche murmured faintly.

"If you had had anything to upset you, I should know better what to think," said Miss Chilcott, surveying the little miserable white face: which turned, all of a sudden and just for a moment, a guilty pink. Blanche was, after all, a very little girl, and not a skilled deceiver. A much more stupid person than Miss Chilcott would have noticed how her eyes went instinctively to a certain drawer, and Miss Chilcott rose and went to that drawer immediately.

"Was *this* what you went out in the rain to get?" she asked, taking out from under tumbled piles of handkerchiefs and ribbons an unmistakable box.

"No, Miss Chilcott! No, *really!*" Blanche protested.

It was a round box of Turkish delight, nearly empty, and there are few more cloying sweets than that. Blanche's midnight troubles were well accounted for.

"Then where did you get it?"

Blanche began to sob.

"Well—it was very wrong of someone to break the rules of the school by giving it to you," said Miss Chilcott, who did not, as has been seen, encourage tale-bearing. "But it was quite as wrong of you to take it, Blanche. You are only a little girl, but you are quite old enough to remember and keep the rule. I am disappointed in you."

She went out very coldly, leaving the miserable Blanche in floods of tears. For it is very bad to feel sick and very trying to be in disgrace, but much worse to know that you deserve both disagreeables.

"No—she's not sickening for anything, I'm thankful to find," Miss Chilcott reported to Miss Pember, displaying her confiscated box. "Nothing worse than this—except that I can't imagine where she can have got it."

"Last night, of course, though I can't think who gave it to her," said Miss Pember promptly.

"No, that was not it. She said so, at once, and it *sounded* quite genuine; and I asked Dorothy, who was quite certain that she was carrying nothing with her when she came in out of the rain. So she would have had no time to hide it, anyhow."

"Very vexing indeed!" said Miss Pember sharply. "But, at any rate, you need not worry any more about infection! Blanche has nothing the matter with her but an ordinary bilious attack, well accounted for, and it's more than three weeks now since the beginning of term—so we are safe!"

The rain, which had cleared off in the night, set in again as persistently as ever about dinner-time; but a brisk walk after morning school had freshened everybody up, and the afternoon rehearsal went with great briskness. People had grasped something of their parts by this time, and realised that they were not just saying "poetry for repetition;" and one or two actors really seemed quite alive and like the people they were supposed to represent. Dorothy knew every word of Helena by this time; she only wished that Rita as Hermia was a little less lifeless, and Miss Pember, coaching, seemed to wish it too.

"Put more life into it, Rita! Try to think that you really *hate* her!"

But that, it appeared, was exactly what Rita couldn't do. She went on making the most injurious speeches in a calm monotone. When Miss Pember again objected and showed her how to do it in the most fiery fashion, Rita only murmured that she was sorry—she had a toothache.

"Go to Nannie and get some iodine, then—now, before your next scene," Miss Pember advised her briskly. "Come along, Fairies! Where's Peaseblossom? Oh, sick in bed, of course. Never mind, I'll take that part."

And she did, with much energy, looking so unlike either the missing Blanche or the real Peaseblossom, that Titania and Bottom had hard work to remember their parts for laughing.

"I'm sorry about your tooth, Rita," said Dorothy, as they all went in to tea.

"Oh, it's not very bad, thanks," Rita rejoined.

But she ate no tea and she went to bed before supper, and the next morning she came down to breakfast with a scarf over her head and round her throat.

"My dear girl, if it is as bad as that I must take you to the dentist this morning," said Miss Chilcott. "You've eaten no breakfast at all—you haven't even drunk your tea. Does the heat make it worse?"

"Yes, Miss Chilcott," murmured Rita indistinctly.

"I'm afraid that sounds very like an abscess," said Miss Chilcott. "But we'll hope not. When did you feel it first?"

"Only yesterday afternoon, Miss Chilcott."

"Well, I'll look at it now, before Prayers," said Miss Chilcott. "Come into my office. Now, take the scarf off and let me see—I won't touch or hurt you. Which tooth is it?"

"It's all down this side," said Rita, slowly unwinding herself and holding her head very stiff.

Miss Chilcott gave a sudden exclamation of horror.

"Rita—*that's* not toothache!"

"Isn't it, Miss Chilcott?" Rita murmured thickly.

"Put the scarf round your head and face at once and go back to bed," said Miss Chilcott. "I'll come up presently."

She had her hand on the telephone as she spoke and to Miss Pember, coming in at that moment, she turned a white and worried face.

"Rita Salmon has got mumps!"

"Mumps! Impossible!" exclaimed Miss Pember crisply.

"I'm afraid there is no doubt about it, but I shan't say anything till the doctor has seen her," said Miss Chilcott. "Oh, dear, and I did think we were safe! It's the *only* thing that takes more than three weeks to come."

"Twenty-eight days quarantine," said Miss Pember, like a Job's comforter.

"I know—and so dreadfully infectious before there is any sign of it at all."

"And Rita everlastingly with the little ones."

"Oh, yes! We shall have a fine crop inside a month," said Miss Pember.

"And then another at the end of another twenty-eight days—*oh!*" said Miss Chilcott, as if she couldn't bear it. "That does for this term, at any rate—"

"And the play," said Miss Pember.

"If it were only the play—! Is that Dr. Ritson? Yes—Miss Chilcott speaking."

And Dr. Ritson came as speedily as his Buick would bring him, and he confirmed the fatal news. There were immediate inquiries up and down the school, and it proved that only five girls out of the whole number had ever had mumps. Miss Chilcott sent out notices to parents and went about looking ten years older; but Miss Pember, getting over the first shock, jerked her head in the air and refused to be depressed.

"We have three weeks before anyone can possibly develop it: so let us make the most of them, *in case* of losing another three after that," she said energetically. "Remember! I shall expect *everyone* to be word-perfect at the next rehearsal!" and this announcement (to many guilty people who had shirked learning their parts) caused such a thrill of horror that an immense wave of industry flowed over the school, and a few specially impressed people were heard murmuring Shakespeare in their sleep. But it served admirably to divert thoughts in general from the possibility of waking up in the morning with a neck like a Roman Emperor. And Dorothy, in particular, found herself acting to Miss Pember's Hermia with a success which surprised herself although she felt some delicacy at first in calling her a juggler and a canker-blossom. But Miss Pember brushed all this away with her accustomed energy.

"You're not Dorothy Grayling, remember, you are Helena. And I am nobody in the world but Hermia—*go on!*"

And Dorothy, thus encouraged, went on; and they acted so well together that there was practically no giggling from either Lysander or Demetrius when she exclaimed of Miss Pember:

> "She was a vixen when she went to school,
>   And though she be but little, she is fierce."

"Very good!" said Hermia, at the end of the scene. "That's the best you've done yet, Dorothy."

And to Miss Chilcott, later in private, she expressed herself even more emphatically.

"Dorothy has really quite a respectable gift of acting, now that she is warming up to it a little; but she never had a chance with that stick of a Rita."

"Rita is not much of an actress, but she remembers her parts wonderfully," said Miss Chilcott.

"Well—for my part, if I could be sure that she hasn't given mumps to half the school, I should be *entirely* reconciled to doing without her for three weeks," said Miss Pember, with her chin in the air.

"You never liked Rita," said Miss Chilcott.

"No. I hate those slow eyes of hers and her quiet murmuring voice. I do my best not to have favourites, or to nurse private aversions," said Miss Pember, with energy, "and I've nothing *against* Rita, if it comes to that, but I really do feel that the school is pleasanter without her!"

"That *is* nonsense," said Miss Chilcott.

"Well—I don't know!" Miss Pember argued. "She has no particular friends, as far as I can see, to miss her—"

"She is very good to the little ones—always."

"Yes. I must admit that," said Miss Pember. "But I can't see that the little ones are any less happy without her. In fact, little Blanche Bates, for one, has looked to me happier and brighter since Rita retired upstairs. And there's Winifred Ray, a little white mouse of a creature ever since she came last term. But to-day I heard her cheeking a girl in the Fifth in the most incredible manner. I had to scold her, of course, but I was really delighted to see that she had any spirit at all. And there's Hester Pyke—not a little one, of course; but she doesn't seem to have groused at all the last day or two."

"Really, for a person who doesn't have private aversions," Miss Chilcott laughed uncontrollably, "you seem to me going pretty far! Do you mean that you *really* account for all this, because poor Rita is shut upstairs in her room with a face like a football?"

Miss Pember laughed too, looking very slightly abashed.

"No. I suppose it's not on account of that. But I should like to believe that it *was!*"

"*Poor* Rita, who is behaving so well—really a model patient under great discomfort," said Miss Chilcott.

"I ought to be ashamed of myself, I know, and I'll send her some grapes when she can eat them," said Miss Pember, with a sudden attack of remorse. "And—if no one catches mumps from her—I'll really try to like her better when she comes down again!"

But she was not called upon to make this noble effort. The very same day that Rita was pronounced free from infection, six other people went into retirement—the three little new girls to whom she had been so kind, and the Captain of the School, and Caroline Cardigan, and Kitty Halliday.

R ITA, reading a letter at breakfast two days after her reappearance, laughed out loud.

"What is it?" inquired her next-door neighbour, with a natural curiosity.

"Only my dear old Aunt Susan," said Rita. "She is always days and weeks behind the times; and now she writes that she is so sorry to hear I am laid up with mumps, and she is sending me a good warm dressing-gown."

Everybody within hearing agreed that it was a little late in the day; but the general opinion was that a new dressing-gown, if pretty, was always worth having.

"Oh, yes. I'm not grumbling, but it *is* funny," said Rita, folding up the letter and putting it in her pocket.

"When is it coming?"

"To-day or to-morrow, I should imagine. She says it is 'just starting'," said Rita, and went on to talk of something else. The subject was, indeed, not interesting enough to take up anyone's attention for long: except, oddly enough, that of Miss Pember, who sat within earshot.

"Now why," she meditated to herself, sitting back and watching the chattering girls, "should Rita have troubled to tell us that? It's not at all exciting; and it's most unlike her to talk about her own affairs or her own people."

There was, however, so obviously no answer to this problem, that Miss Pember gave herself a little shake as she rose from the table.

"Miss Chilcott is quite right—I *don't* like Rita Salmon," she told herself sharply. "But that is no excuse for imagining things against her without the slightest foundation.—I'll just notice whether a dressing-gown *does* come for her, though."

And the dressing-gown came in due course, a very luxurious heavy woollen one, of an unusual dull blue. The other girls admired it enviously.

"The box was such a weight, I didn't think it *could* be a dressing-gown, Rita," said Ella Bass, the Paul Pry of the school.

Rita changed colour very slightly. It certainly was an annoying comment.

"Well, you see you were mistaken for once, Beer," she drawled annoyingly in answer, for none knew better how intensely Ella hated her obvious nickname. "Just feel the weight for yourself, if you aren't satisfied; and as a matter of fact, my dear old aunt sent me some books as well, to read while I was in quarantine. Perhaps you'd like to borrow one? She recommended this particularly!"

She held out a dull green book, very old-fashioned in appearance, called *The Schoolgirl's Good Resolution;* and a ripple of laughter ran round the room. Ella Bass, who was no reader at the best of times, turned a fiery red and retreated in discomfiture. ... It was a curious fact—Miss Pember might have noted it if she had been in the room, but she wasn't—that people who annoyed Rita nearly always were discomfited, sooner or later.

Dorothy was present at this little scene, but she was not one of the laughers; she was, in fact, wrapped in her own meditations, and they were not particularly pleasant ones. It was a Tuesday, and yesterday the F.G. notice had appeared as before on the Notice Board—mysteriously there, when everyone came downstairs, mysteriously gone before any mistresses were likely to pass that way. And Dorothy didn't *want* to go and meet Rita by the cloak-room door after tea this evening. The more she thought about it, the more certain she was of that, and the less she saw how to get out of going. That silly little business of the scrap of paper had stuck in her mind. It had seemed so absolutely senseless; and she was a sensible girl, who didn't like being despatched to do silly things with no reason given. Yet—well, she supposed she would have to go. There didn't seem any way out of it, and she had a shrewd impression that Rita was not a good person to offend.

"Good evening, Jonah!"

Rita had not kept her waiting this time. She had a little parcel in her hand.

"There's no F.G. business for you to do this time," she said at once, making Dorothy flush uncomfortably. (How *did* Rita read one's thoughts in this uncanny manner? But perhaps she had observed an uneasy glance at the little parcel). "All I have to say is, that there will be a General Meeting on Friday."

Well! that was not so bad. Dorothy was distinctly curious to know who were her fellow-members, and she was relieved not to have to throw any more papers about.

"Where? And what time?" she asked.

"We always have to have them at night, of course," said Rita in a matter-of-fact way. "But no one seems to find any difficulty about keeping awake till the right time. Half-past twelve, in the bath-room on your landing."

She paused, but Dorothy had no comment to make. It was certainly rather dismaying to have to lie awake from ten o'clock for two hours and a half, but, if other people found it easy to do, she supposed she could do the same.

"This is what you wear," said Rita, handing her the little parcel.

"What I—wear?"

"Over your ordinary clothes, of course," Rita smiled at her amiably. "You never heard, did you, of a Secret Society that hadn't some sort of badge or disguise? Be careful not to leave it about where any outsiders might see it. Good-bye, Jonah."

She walked away in her quiet fashion, and Dorothy was left with her parcel. She was extremely curious to know what it contained, but it wasn't safe to open it there and then—anyone might come by. She must wait for the safe seclusion of her cubicle at bedtime, for it was against the rules to go there in the day. Perhaps a state of mental curiosity is not very compatible with preparation; for certainly Dorothy was much slower at hers than usual that night and was left behind by most of the other girls when they went off for half-an-hour's dancing before supper.

"What a long time you've been, Dorothy!—Why, you're not doing your Scripture, are you?"

"Yes, of course. Why not?"

"There's no need to give it in till next week. Don't you know that Miss Chilcott will be away on Friday?"

Dorothy looked up quickly.

"Miss Chilcott away?"

"Yes—some meeting at Cambridge. She won't be back till quite late on Saturday."

Dorothy very slowly began to put her books away, thinking hard. There wasn't, of course, any object in doing work now for Friday week, but that was not what kept her thoughts so busy. Miss Chilcott would be away on Friday—right away, with no possibility of coming back unexpectedly, and that was the night chosen for the F.G. meeting. ...

Dorothy didn't like it; and, thinking it over more, she liked it still less. The chances were, of course, all against Miss Chilcott's approving in any case of a midnight meeting; but there was no actual *rule* forbidding such a thing, and bath-rooms were not out of bounds as were other girls' bedrooms. In an ordinary way, members of the F.G. would just be taking an ordinary chance of being found out and probably punished, and that was fair enough. But, with Miss Chilcott away for that one night, it seemed—mean.

Dorothy went down and watched the other girls dancing, refusing to dance herself. She was still in a brown study as she ate her supper, and she went up to bed very thoughtfully indeed, with Rita's mysterious little parcel in her hand. Perhaps the contents of that might in some way help her to solve her difficulty.

She drew her cubicle curtain very close and untied the string.

Inside there was just a piece of black silk, and as Dorothy shook it out in bewilderment, she saw that it was most neatly hemmed and made up, with two largish holes beautifully blanket-stitched at one end. Turning it about and staring at it, she suddenly saw what it was.

The holes were eye-holes, like those in an executioner's mask, and when she fitted it on, she found that it *was* a mask, fastened on to a sort of caplike veil that covered her hair entirely. Looking in the glass, she would not have known herself—it might have been anybody staring back at her through those holes in the black silk. She might have been a person out of the Inquisition, or a first cousin of the Man in the Iron Mask. It was really an extraordinarily clever disguise—so simple, and so absolutely successful. For the first time, Dorothy felt that she really did belong to a Secret Society, and that it was rather fun and rather exciting, and—and perhaps there was no harm in the midnight meeting, after all. But she was not quite sure about that. She lay awake in bed for a long time, thinking and wondering and coming to no conclusion. Rita was in the Sixth, and presumably she had been at St. Madern's for a long time: one *ought* to be able to trust her not to ask anyone to do unsuitable things. And Dorothy was a new girl and not very well acquainted with the ways of the school, and it would seem—well, awful cheek—if she made a fuss: also she might be called a prig, which would be extremely hateful. She fell asleep at last with her mind still full of unpleasant doubts.

Wednesday passed without events.

So did Thursday.

On Friday morning Rita said to her casually, as they met in a passage:

"By the way, I forgot to tell you. Bring your tooth-glass to-night, will you?"

"My—tooth-glass?" stammered Dorothy, much taken aback.

"Yes. Don't forget!"

Rita nodded and went quickly on, and the opportunity was lost; for Dorothy was still petrified with astonishment and had had no time to arrange what she wanted to say—if indeed she really wanted to say it. No other chance occurred all day; and tea came, and preparation, and supper and—bedtime.

There was no difficulty about keeping awake. At any rate Dorothy lay with her eyes wide open and her heart beating rather fast, and she had to own that her excitement was more than half pleasant. A mystery is always thrilling; and she did badly want to wear that black silk mask and find out at last what the F.G. really was and how many people belonged to it. In spite of being so wide awake, she lay as still as possible: for it would be extraordinarily awkward if Ada Ling, in the next cubicle, heard her stirring soon after the clock struck twelve. It was a piece of luck that Caroline had retired to the sickrooms; at least there was only one person whom she must not disturb.

Eleven.

It was not a cold night, that was a blessing. And another was that the house was central-heated, so that even the bath-room would be comfortably warm. Dorothy's dressing-gown was thick and cosy, and the delightful slippers, like furry grey mice, that had been a Christmas present from her mother, were the warmest things in the world—how the other girls admired them!—and quite soundless. Rita would wear her new dressing-gown, of course. … What a jolly Christmas it had been, and how wonderful it was to go to church again, and look at the decorations that her own hands had helped to put up—why, she had even been allowed to stand on a ladder! It was sad, of course, that she couldn't go to any dances—but next year. …

Half-past eleven.

Dorothy turned over excitedly; and then was afraid that she had made a noise, and lay mouse-still again. What a mercy it was that Ada was such a heavy sleeper! There was not a sound from her cubicle. Dorothy hoped that Caroline—a kind, pleasant creature—was not suffering much upstairs. People said that mumps were perfectly beastly. … What an awful thing it would be if another batch fell at the end of this quarantine—quite likely, of course. It would ruin the whole term. There would be no play. The thing might even run on into the Easter holidays—which weren't so very long, in any case—and how unspeakably awful that would be! Fancy staying in a sick-room at school, with a face like a football, instead of ecstatically going home! It didn't bear thinking of. … In another hour she would know all that there was to be known about the F.G., and what *could* it be? How many members were there? It might be half the school, it might—it might be only Rita and herself, after all, and the whole thing might be a hoax! That was a most thoroughly unpleasant idea, and Dorothy hastily dismissed it from her mind. … What could be the use of a tooth-glass? She must be sure not to forget to bring it back again, after the meeting was over. Suppose she left it in the bath-room—and couldn't do her teeth in the morning—and the housemaid found it there … One tooth-glass was very like another. Would the … whole … school … be … collected … and … asked. …

Twelve long, slow strokes boomed out through the silent house, and Dorothy started up in a fright. She had actually been dropping asleep, after all!

The fright had roused her so thoroughly that there was no fear of that any more. Besides, in a few minutes she would have to get up and dress. It wasn't easy to dress in the dark, though she had carefully left everything in perfect order, so that her hand might fall on everything in turn without the least difficulty. What an awful thing if, at that crucial moment, she couldn't find one stocking! And she would never dare to open her drawer—which always creaked a little—to find another.

She slipped, with extreme caution, out of bed, and stood fixed for a moment, with a horrible conviction that she had heard Ada moving on the other side of the curtain. But no. Listening with all her ears, there was nothing but perfect silence.

Even with everything laid in perfect order, it is not too easy to dress in the dark. Dorothy found herself putting things on upside down and inside out. One of those fatal stockings did betray her, after all, and had to be scrambled for all down the bottom edge of the curtain before she found it finally under a chair. And then, putting on one of the mouse-shoes, she dropped it, and it fell with a soft thud— the sort of sound that would be quite inaudible by day, but it sounded like a young earthquake to the dismayed Dorothy. She stood listening again, and was perfectly certain, this time, that Ada *had* moved.

Two minutes of immovable silence, and then she absolutely couldn't hold herself so stiff and silent any more—and besides, time was getting on. She mustn't, of all things, be late, and it was impossible to tell exactly how near all the invisible clocks were to striking the half-hour. Very cautiously she drew aside her curtain— not running it along the rings, which were sure to jingle, but lifting it up from the bottom—and slipped out under it. She was the nearest to the door, and that was a mercy.

The next moment she was back again in her cubicle. She had forgotten the black mask, and what a terrible thing that would have been!

It was the worst thing of all to adjust in the dark. Dorothy had to feel with her fingers just how far it came down over her face—to the tip of her nose, leaving her mouth and chin free—and whether the veil part hung smoothly down behind and was not caught up anywhere. And now, indeed, she must hurry if she was not to be late, for the veil business had taken an appreciable number of minutes. Out under the curtain again, touching the door with her finger-tips. …

It said much for the self-control of two girls that two long screams did not break the stillness of the midnight house; for Dorothy's groping fingers, searching for the handle, met suddenly other fingers intent upon the same design.

There were two very distinct gasps. Then Ada said: "Oh, it's *you!*" at the exact moment when Dorothy said the same words. Neither of them had anything more to say, and neither ever knew whose hand it was that actually opened the door.

Outside in the passage they stood staring at each other for a minute in the dim light that was always left burning all night long. Shrouded in the F.G. black veil, either of them might have been anybody: it was an amazingly good disguise. There was, of course, nothing to say; and neither of them would have dared to say it if there had been. With noiseless steps they crept softly along the corridor, and, when a distant door very gently opened and shut again, both started with a frightful sense of guilt and stood quite still, staring. But it was only another veiled figure that appeared suddenly from nowhere without seeing them, and turned off in the direction of the bath-room. So far, they were safe.

Did ever half the length of a corridor and the width of a small landing seem such an immense distance? Dorothy thought not, and it is probable that Ada was entirely of the same opinion.

The bath-room door stood ajar, but not a sound came from inside it. Ada pushed it open and they slipped in; and instantly the door shut softly behind them.

"Good morning, Jonah! Good morning, Jonah!" said Rita.

She was the only person there who was not veiled. Some half-dozen mysterious figures stood uneasily about the room, which was large for a bath-room, and contained a piano on which people practised; and on the piano-stool Rita sat at her ease, wearing her new dressing-gown. Dorothy, glancing hastily round, saw that it was quite impossible to recognise anyone, and was thankful. She was also quite positively sure, for the first time, that she had made the mistake of her life in coming, or in ever joining the F.G. at all.

The clock struck, and everyone started violently, with a conscious guilt—everyone, that is, but Rita, who was perfectly composed.

"All admirably punctual!" she said, with her slow smile. "Now—as we don't want to be too late, remembering that breakfast is in about seven hours' time—we had better begin at once. Will everybody please sit down?"

There was nothing to sit on but the floor and everybody accordingly sat on that, without a word.

"Glasses, please!" said Rita, and collected one from each person present, arranging them neatly on a tray which stood on the top of the piano.

"Now," she said, with another slow smile, "Will everyone please begin? Help yourselves! and please finish *everything*—or it will be such a bother to dispose of afterwards."

Dorothy (who had been staring round at the veiled company, and trying to make up her mind whether the little one in the corner was Blanche Bates) looked elsewhere for the first time, and perceived that the bath-room wore a very unusual guise. The top of the bath had been covered in with a board or something of the sort; and over this was a railway rug, making an improvised table for a most magnificent feast, of the kind that may be eaten fairly elegantly with the fingers alone. Nuts and dates and figs, crystallised fruits of the most expensive kinds, shortbreads, biscuits of various sorts, mostly sugary, chocolates and other sweets. It was a sight to rejoice the heart of any schoolgirl—or doctor.

"There are two pairs of nutcrackers," said Rita. "*Do* get on, someone! I shan't ask you again."

One or two people began timidly to help themselves and others quickly followed suit, while Rita, always smiling, mixed lemonade powder with water from a bath-room jug, filled the glasses and handed them round.

"Pass the spoons on, please. I've only got three, I'm afraid," she said.

The air was filled with the crunching of biscuits, the cracking of nuts, the rustling sound of silver paper being stripped off the best chocolates. The well-filled plates—picnic plates of cardboard—began to lighten surprisingly.

"Come, Jonah! You're eating nothing!" said Rita, and passed a plate of mixed biscuits to Dorothy, who was sitting with her glass in her hand neither eating nor drinking. It was indeed a sight to melt the stoutest heart; sponge biscuits, and gingerbreads, and biscuits filled with cream and coated with sugar, and others glistening with chocolate. Rita smiled afresh, very persuasively, as she held it invitingly out.

"Take several! two of each kind, at least," she said.

Dorothy stood up suddenly. She had had her doubts for days past: she was quite sure now.

"I'm awfully sorry, Rita, but—no, thank you!" she said.

"What! Not well?" said Rita. "What a pity!"

"No. It's not that. I'm quite well, thank you," said Dorothy, stumbling over her words and feeling herself turn scarlet under her mask.

"Well—why not, then?" asked Rita, standing quite still and looking at her.

Though she wore no mask, the fixed smile in itself looked like a kind of mask, it was so unchanging, and so hard.

"There's—there's the rule against sweets on any day except Sunday," said Dorothy.

"Well—no one could call this *day!*" said Rita, with a laugh and a glance at the drawn blinds.

Dorothy suddenly found herself less frightened, perhaps because she was growing angry.

"That's nonsense," she said, quite boldly. "Besides, there's the other rule about not having any sort of food from home."

The cracking of nuts had quite ceased, and there was no more rustling of silver paper. It was uncanny—almost frightening—to see all those eyes staring at her from behind their expressionless masks.

"Well—any more?" asked Rita.

"Yes!" said Dorothy, quite bold now and quite sure that she was in the right. "And I think it's worse to choose the only night when Miss Chilcott is away. If she had been at home, it wouldn't have felt quite so—mean."

There was a little uneasy stir round the bath-room. One or two people furtively put down half-eaten biscuits. Somebody took a sip of lemonade and choked over it, very disconcertingly.

"Dear—me!" said Rita, in a slow drawl. "This is quite a new point of view for the F.G.! And doesn't it strike you as being a little bit—ungrateful?"

"I'm *sorry*, Rita!" said Dorothy, struck with remorse. "I think it was perfectly ripping of you to give a feast like this, and I don't suppose you—or anybody else—ever thought of it in the way I've said. Or you wouldn't have done it."

"No," drawled Rita. "We had to wait for our newest member to tell us that. I don't think any of the rest of us are—prigs."

The ugly word stuck and stung, and Dorothy flushed scarlet again. There didn't seem anything more to say.

Rita suddenly burst out laughing.

"Don't be an idiot, Jonah!" she said. "Can't you join in a harmless little bit of fun like this? I know you've never been at a boarding-school before, but surely you must know that this sort of thing is *always* done in the best schools! Sit down again and don't be a dramatic lunatic, and try these biscuits—the fan-shaped ones are the best, I think."

It was very much harder to resist this forgiving and friendly appeal. It took a great effort for Dorothy to lean forward and pour the contents of her untasted glass into the nearest glass that was empty.

"I haven't touched this," she said. "Rita—I'm most awfully sorry, and I do thank you tremendously for inviting me to come. But—I can't stay."

She went quickly out, with her sticky, empty glass in her hand; and the laughter that followed her was the hardest thing of all to bear. She had no idea how many laughed, or how many were left sitting still and uncomfortable. She only knew that tears suddenly blinded her eyes and streamed down her cheeks. She tore off her mask as she went.

"I'll give this back to Rita tomorrow: and I'm done with the F.G.!" she said.

CHAPTER XI

Rehearsing

THE clock struck half-past one just as Ada softly turned the handle of the door and came creeping in, but Dorothy was not asleep. She lay very still, however; and Ada for her part crept like a mouse about her work of undressing and getting into bed again. When the dressing-bell rang—after what seemed like next to no time—they both got up again in perfect silence. Usually a pleasant little rain of remarks streamed from cubicle to cubicle. The dead silence, broken only by unromantic sounds of washing and dressing, was extremely uncomfortable. Both were truly thankful, at breakfast time, to hear that their roommate, Caroline, had been unjustly accused of mumps, and would return to them that night after her period of probation. She would, of course, have plenty to say about it, and she was blissfully ignorant of the F.G. fiasco.

The pocket of Dorothy's drill-slip was bulging most uncomfortably, but she could not afford to lose any opportunity that offered of returning her property to Rita. One occurred, mercifully, before more than ten people had observed the bulge and asked her what in the world she had got there.

"Rita—will you take this back, please?"

Dorothy was a little out of breath—partly because she had had to run down the cloak-room corridor to catch Rita, who looked at the little parcel without offering to take it.

"What is this?" she inquired, with perfect coolness.

"You *know* what it is!" said Dorothy: and indeed there was every reason why she should, for it was packed in its original paper and shape and folds. "And—thank you very much, Rita—but I don't want to belong to the F.G. any more."

"The F.G. are born, not made," said Rita, more coolly than ever. "You can't help yourself, Jonah. Once an F.G., always an F.G."

"You can't *make* me belong if I don't want to," said Dorothy, half alarmed and half angry.

"What about the Freemasons?" said Rita, and went smiling on her way.

And Dorothy was left with that hateful little parcel in her hand. She hid it in her desk all day, and at night she buried it deep under everything at the bottom of her bottom drawer, but that was not at all the same thing as getting rid of it.

The rehearsals of the play were, of course, very much handicapped by the absence of so many actors in quarantine, and that day Miss Tuke, who usually took Kitty Halliday's part of Bottom, was laid up with a headache and could not appear. Miss Pember looked round her in despair.

"Such an important part! And it makes everyone act so badly if it's just read, now that we have got so far!" she lamented. She looked with a lack-lustre eye at one girl after another, and seemed to think that each would do a little worse than the one before her, and nobody was very anxious to fill the gap. It was bad enough to be hauled over the coals in one's own part, without getting raged at for not knowing a part that was somebody else's.

Dorothy, after a good deal of hesitation, raised a modest voice. It wasn't for her, a mere newcomer, to make such an offer, but, if none of the elder girls would—and she *had* seen the play acted, and her memory was not so bad—

"I think I know some of it, Miss Pember," she hinted modestly.

"Oh, well! I suppose that's better than nothing!" said Miss Pember, with resignation. "Come along—*Scene* 2: *Enter Quince, Snug, Bottom, Flute, Snout, and Starveling.*—Bottom's is the second speech—here's the book."

"I think I know the beginning of it," said Dorothy.

Miss Pember stared at her.

"Oh, well, so much the better! Go on as far as you can without the book, then. It makes it easier for the others."

Now Dorothy had not only seen the play acted, and read it with her mother: she had taken an interest in other scenes besides her own, and had seen it now rehearsed a good many times, and had made several private mental notes that she didn't think Kitty Halliday at all a good Bottom. Also her memory was remarkably good. She went through the scene, therefore, with great success, quite enjoying herself and only requiring to be prompted twice.

"Why didn't you tell me that you had acted Bottom before?" asked Miss Pember sharply.

"But I haven't, Miss Pember!" said Dorothy, aggrieved.

"Well, you seem to know something about it, at any rate.—Come along, Puck! Don't waste time!"

Dorothy sat and watched with interest, waiting for her turn as Helena, a part which she didn't like half so well. Her Demetrius was such a stick, and she hated the lovering; it made her feel so foolish. Much more amusing to have a part where one was meant to make people laugh, and could take a pride and satisfaction in doing so.

"Now, be ready, fairies, for goodness' sake, to come on with Titania," said Miss Pember, who, it must be owned, was not in the best of tempers. "One, two. three—where's Peaseblossom?"

"Please, Miss Pember, she's in bed."

"Sick *again*? *Well!*" said Miss Pember, most sharply of all. "She's not very important, luckily; but what a little pig—and how does she manage it? ... I'll read her lines. Go *on!*"

Dorothy felt herself hot all over. She knew well enough why Blanche (who was Peaseblossom) was in bed, she wondered how many other people in the room knew it too. But she didn't dare look round and see, partly because she did not wish to draw any unnecessary attention on herself, partly because she would really rather not know. ... So the little masked thing in the corner of the bath-room *had* been Blanche, as she suspected at the time.

She needed a good deal more prompting in Bottom's next scene, because her mind was wandering in quite a different direction; and Miss Pember was less pleased with her. But when she came on again as Helena, she had learnt her part so very well that the repetition of it was mechanical: even Miss Pember could find no fault there.

"Wake up, though, Dorothy!" she said. "You're word-perfect, of course, and that is a great deal, but it's not everything by any means; and you generally act a great deal better than that."

"I'm sorry, Miss Pember," Dorothy apologised meekly, and

shook herself together, and firmly drove the F.G. and all its doings from her mind. Here was her quarrelling scene, and that was much more to her taste than love-making.

"*Re-enter Hermia*," read Miss Pember, and subsequently, when the long scene was over, "Very good! You have never done that with so much spirit before."

But there was something a little odd in her tone, and in her look too, as she stared first at Rita and then at Dorothy: who, for her part, accepted the praise complacently enough. It was quite true. Rita, usually a very inanimate player, had been much more alive than usual—quite spiteful in some of her cutting speeches—and that made it enormously easier to play up to her. Even the stick-like Demetrius and Lysander had really had to hold her back when she threatened Helena, instead of just putting a couple of fingers on her in their usual fashion.

> "Why will you suffer her to flout me thus?
> Let me come to her!"

Yes, it had been necessary for Helena to step back very quickly at that, for Hermia really did look as though she meant to scratch her face; and that, of course, was just as it should be. Dorothy found herself subsequently going on with Bottom's part in the most spirited fashion, and again needing hardly any prompting at all. In fact, she had never enjoyed any rehearsal so much.

Miss Pember, her duties in that direction over, went straight to Miss Chilcott.

"I put on Dorothy Grayling in Kitty's part to-day, as she said she knew something about it. As a matter of fact, she knew it practically all through—she has a very remarkable memory. And she acts Bottom a hundred per cent better than Kitty. I wish you'd give her the part!"

"We can't possibly change, so late in the day," said Miss Chilcott, a good deal surprised.

"We *could*. The term is only half over."

"And it would be very unfair to Kitty, who has already had to learn a long part—"

"She doesn't anything like know it!" argued Miss Pember, with energy.

"She's probably devoting some of her present abundant leisure to getting it perfect," smiled Miss Chilcott. "Time hangs very heavy on hand in the sick-rooms, I'm afraid."

"Well—I assure you that the play would go incomparably better—"

"But Kitty couldn't play Helena. She is no good at all in a serious part."

"Or any other," Miss Pember muttered rebelliously.

"Besides—I really hesitated a good deal, as you know, before giving a new girl so important a part as Helena," said Miss Chilcott. "I don't see how I *can* promote her to Bottom, over the head of a Sixth Form girl. It would look like a terrible piece of favouritism—and you know I always do my very best to avoid that."

"I think the play should come first," said Miss Pember with her sharp chin in the air.

"Not before the good of the school," Miss Chilcott smiled at her.

"The ... good ... of ... the ... school!" Miss Pember repeated very slowly. "I wonder what you would say if I told you what I think you should *really* do, for the good of the school!"

"Please don't! for I am sure it is something most disagreeable," said Miss Chilcott in haste, though she smiled still.

"You never did like disagreeables, did you?" said Miss Pember, with a little sharp nod at her. "Well—so I am to make the best of a bad job, with Kitty as Bottom? And Dorothy is to be wasted on Helena!"

"I'm afraid so," said Miss Chilcott, almost apologetically.

She was really relieved when Miss Pember had whisked out of the room with a little sharp click of the door. Quite an invaluable mistress, of course, and such an old friend, but a little difficult sometimes—and so very much inclined to like some girls immensely, and to dislike others quite as much, without any apparent reason!

CHAPTER XII

WINIFRED

"BR'R! It ees cold!" shivered Mademoiselle, coming out of the dining-room after tea. "And I left my leetle grey co-at in ze dressing-room—"

"I'll get it for you, Mademoiselle," Dorothy offered at once, and ran quickly down the passage.

The mistresses had a little dressing-room inside the bigger one that belonged to the girls; and Dorothy, with a secret chuckle, thought as she entered it that, if mistresses had Order Marks, there were several due here. A hat was on the floor, and a small thick coat hung up anyhow—those were Miss Pember's, for she always flew in and out in a desperate hurry, and no one else wore such a child's size. But Miss Tyrrell, who taught needlework and was most particular about neatly-finished seams, really ought to know better than to hang her coat by the sleeve because the loop had come undone! A pair of gloves was on the floor, but those might be anybody's. And—where *was* Mademoiselle's little grey co-at?

Dorothy hunted on peg after peg, finally running her prey to earth—literally—in a most obscure corner on the ground. The search had taken some time. As she turned with the "co-at" in her hand, a sudden voice outside made her pause.

"No—no! I won't—I really *won't!*"

There was an answer of some sort, but it was quite indistinguishable; and Dorothy suddenly realised that she had been vaguely aware, as she hunted, of a murmur of voices not very far off. Who could be arguing like that, just outside the cloak-room—after tea? ...

Dorothy suddenly stood quite still, forgetting Mademoiselle altogether.

Outside the cloak-room after tea.

It wasn't Tuesday, which had been her own appointed day. It

was Wednesday—obviously somebody else's appointed day. And somebody else was being given an F.G. job to do and quite evidently didn't like it. Dorothy, straining her ears, was quite sure that the slow murmur now going on was Rita's voice; but that was of course only to be expected. Apparently the other speaker had been warned to be quieter, for no more words were distinguishable. If they had been, it would have been difficult to know what to do, since eavesdropping is always hateful. As it was, Dorothy stood still where she was, most uncomfortable from every point of view. Mademoiselle would be wondering why her coat did not come—might even come in search of it herself: but that was a small matter. The really horrid thing was the feeling, which was growing more and more upon Dorothy, that something underhand and disagreeable was at work in the school, doing real harm and quite impossible to get at.

The voices suddenly ceased and there was a sound of footsteps—rather cautious footsteps; and Dorothy, with a sudden impulse, went quickly through both cloak-rooms and looked after the speakers. It was dangerous, of course; Rita might look back—and Dorothy was becoming more and more imbued with the idea that Rita was not a person to annoy. On the other hand, it did seem eminently desirable to know who the person was who had been given a job to do and didn't like it.

Both figures were moving quickly and almost out of sight. But it was Rita without a doubt, and—the other girl turned her face at the corner, just where the light fell on it and Dorothy could see her distinctly. It was Winifred Ray, a delicate, nervous creature, not nearly so high up in the school as she should have been for her age, rather stupid, very easily frightened or hurt. Just the sort of girl, in fact, to get into the clutches of the F.G. and helplessly hate it, without having either the strength or the wit to free herself. Dorothy felt herself going hot with indignation.

"Here is your coat, Mademoiselle. I am sorry I was so long, but it had fallen down and I couldn't find it," she apologised, in her admirable French.

And Mademoiselle, thanking her, made a little jest about thinking that the messenger must have been knitting a new one instead; and Dorothy laughed dutifully and went on into the preparation room.

She was rather early; but Winifred was already there, bending over her desk and hard at work.

Could anything be said? If anything, what?

As Dorothy hesitated over this question, feeling the hopelessness of the whole thing, other girls came in and the opportunity was lost. But, keeping an eye on Winifred for the rest of the evening as opportunity served, she thought her looking white and worried. It was not only imagination, either, for Miss Pember commented on it after supper.

"You don't look well, Winifred. Have you got one of your headaches coming on?"

"No, thank you, Miss Pember," Winifred answered, in rather an unsteady voice, and she flushed and paled uneasily. … She had eaten hardly any supper, and had hardly spoken to anyone.

"Look here, Winifred," Dorothy said bluntly, making an opportunity to walk by her as they all went to bed, "if you haven't got a headache, there's something the matter! Can I do anything?"

Winifred, looking at her with scared eyes, said nothing.

"I'll do anything I can, and love to," Dorothy urged. "Do tell me what it is. I hate to see you looking like that."

"I—there's nothing to tell," said Winifred, in a faint voice.

"That's nonsense," said Dorothy.—"You needn't tell me, of course, if you don't want to; but if you've any sense at all, you'll tell *someone*."

"I—can't!"

"I thought you said there was nothing to tell?" said Dorothy, still looking straight at her.

"There isn't—there isn't!" Winifred began to babble, looking thoroughly frightened.

"That's *nonsense*," said Dorothy again, with great firmness. "Either you've done something and you're afraid of being found out, or somebody is being beastly to you. Now … which is it?"

Winifred gave a little gasp.

"Or—perhaps it's *both*?" said Dorothy.

She had great hopes that this last shot had gone home; for Winifred began to sob in a helpless, terrified way, like a child who is afraid to cry out loud, and with her sobs there came broken words about "if I were like you"—"if only I dared"—And then suddenly, at that hopeful moment, Rita came in her slow way along the passage, looking steadily at them, and Winifred bolted into her own room—they had been standing outside the open door—like a frightened rabbit.

"On somebody else's passage *again?*" said Rita to Dorothy, pausing with a queer little smile.

"I don't know what you mean!" Dorothy flung back at her.

"Well—this isn't the way to your room, is it. And—"

"It isn't the way to yours either!" said Dorothy, flaming with defiance and really feeling as if she didn't care *what* she said.

"—And it isn't the first time you have been found in other girls' rooms, is it?" Rita finished her sentence smoothly, as if she had not heard the interruption. And she walked, soft-footed, on her way, only throwing back one last remark:

"Good night, Winifred! I hope your head will be all right in the morning."

"Do get into bed as fast as ever you can," Dorothy urged the poor pale frightened thing, standing just inside the door as if she did not dare to move. And Winifred started like a person waking out of some unpleasant dream, and murmured a miserable word of thanks and began dismally to undress. It kept Dorothy awake for quite a considerable time—say a quarter of an hour—thinking about her and wondering and being helplessly compassionate.

If Winifred did get quickly into bed, she looked next morning as if sleep had taken a long time in coming to her. But she anxiously denied all suggestions of headaches and doses, and worked feverishly away at her lessons—she was one of those slow girls who have to work about twice as long as other people to reach the same result with the utmost energy.

"I don't like the looks of her," Miss Chilcott said, rather uneasily, to Miss Pember after dinner. "No, I know mumps doesn't start that way! But I wish you would keep an eye on her, and see how she seems at tea-time. I really wish I were not going over to that tiresome party at Collingfield this afternoon."

"Nonsense!" said Miss Pember crisply. "You hardly ever leave the school in term-time, and it will do you good. Do you think I'm not capable of putting Winifred to bed if it's necessary and sticking a thermometer in her mouth? But I don't think you need worry in that way. I don't believe, myself, that it is *anything* physical."

"What do you mean?" Miss Chilcott asked anxiously.

But Miss Pember only answered crisply that she would be late for rehearsal if she stayed another minute, and whisked out of the room.

It *was* refreshing to get right away from the school atmosphere and its worries for a couple of hours, among people who never mentioned mumps or returned lessons or the taking of temperatures. Miss Chilcott enjoyed herself more than she had expected, and stayed longer than she meant; it was six o'clock when she left the little country town, seven miles away, and drove off in her little car, and it was a dark, wet evening, depressing and dismal. She was delayed an extra few minutes by giving a compassionate lift to a foolish fellow-guest who had rashly come out without an umbrella, and after that it was necessary to drive slowly and with caution, having due regard to the possibility of a skid and the possibility of invisible pedestrians in the little country lanes—not that it was the sort of night that anyone would walk abroad who might stay comfortably at home. Miss Chilcott enjoyed her drive so little that she was sincerely thankful to see the lights of St. Madern's in the distance and to know that she had only one more bit of dark lane before she turned into her own avenue.

At that very moment the possible accident so very nearly happened that Miss Chilcott turned cold with fright. Someone, quite invisible in the darkness, suddenly slipped from under the very wheels of the car, as it seemed, with a squeak of fright.

"Who is it? I do trust you are not hurt!" Miss Chilcott called out anxiously, pulling up and leaning out to look.

There was certainly someone there, in the ditch by the roadside, someone who neither answered nor moved. Miss Chilcott, more frightened than before—though she had been going so very slowly and carefully that she couldn't feel in any way guilty—turned her powerful little pocket-torch in that direction.

"*Who is it?*" she said, with a sudden new sharp note in her voice: for it is unnatural for the victim of any motor-accident to cover her face with her hands and cower still deeper into a very muddy ditch.

There was no answer; and Miss Chilcott, who could be almost as quick as Miss Pember on occasion, sprang out of the car and took the cowering figure by the shoulder, drawing her into the light of the car-lamps. She was justified in this vigorous measure, for the light of the little torch had unmistakably revealed the St. Madern's green uniform.

"Now—who is it?" she said, in the voice of authority that brooks no disobedience. "What—*you*, Winifred?"

The woebegone face revealed in the light of the lamps was white and horrified, with tears of terror streaming down it. The green uniform was soaked.

"Get in!" said Miss Chilcott shortly; and drove on to the house considerably faster than was advisable on such a night.

The hall was empty, that was a blessing. In the bright light there, Miss Chilcott surveyed for a moment the sorry figure before her.

"Go up to your room, and get off those things as quickly as you can and get into bed," she directed briefly. "I shall be up in five minutes."

"Well! did you have a nice time and do you feel freshened up?" Miss Pember inquired cheerfully, appearing the very next moment. "Why—what's the matter?"

"I've no time to tell you now," was Miss Chilcott's grim answer. "What about Winifred?"

"She did confess to a headache at tea, and I sent her to bed," said Miss Pember briskly. "But she had no temperature. I'm sure it's nothing."

"You sent her to bed?"

"Yes. Wasn't that right?"

"Perfectly," said Miss Chilcott. "But it doesn't account for my finding her in the lane outside just now, fully dressed and wet through!"

"Winifred! In the lane!" Miss Pember repeated incredulously.

"Yes," said Miss Chilcott. "I am going up to see her now, as soon as I have taken my coat off. Wait for me in the office, will you?"

The guilty one was in bed safe enough, and there was a little heap of wet clothes on a chair which Miss Chilcott scanned with a practised eye. Yes—she would not be taking any more outdoor walks to-night. Those things would all be sent down to be dried before she was left alone again.

"Now, Winifred—what were you doing out of doors at this time of night?"

Winifred sat up in bed, shivering from head to foot.

"Lie down again," said Miss Chilcott practically. "You don't want to run any *more* risk of a chill. Now—tell me!"

"I—went to post a letter," Winifred mumbled, through chattering teeth.

"To—post a letter!"

"Yes, Miss Chilcott."

"But you know perfectly well that that is against the rules. All letters have to be posted in the house-box, so that I can see the addresses."

"Yes, Miss Chilcott."

"Then why did you break this particularly strict rule?"

Winifred only shivered in silence.

"Where did you post it?"

"I—I meant to give it to the postman. But I missed him, and I had to go on to the letter-box in the wall—by the white gate."

"But that is a mile away!"

"Yes, Miss Chilcott."

"What was this letter, that had to be posted like that?"

Winifred turned a little whiter, if that were possible, but lay silent.

"You say you meant to give it to the postman. Have you ever done such a thing before?"

"Yes, Miss Chilcott."

"More than once?"

"No, Miss Chilcott—*really* only once before!"

"Who was the letter addressed to?" asked Miss Chilcott: for even a head mistress can forget the stricter rules of grammar in moments of stress.

Winifred sobbed and shivered.

"Come, Winifred! You can only make the best of a bad job by confessing honestly."

"To—to—"

"Yes?" said Miss Chilcott.

"I *can't* tell you!" sobbed Winifred, and buried her face in the pillow.

"Why not? You must know!"

If silence gives consent, Winifred gave consent. Besides, it is very rare to post a letter whose address one does not know.

"Then tell me—at once."

"I *daren't!*" Winifred sobbed hopelessly.

"You *daren't?* Why?" asked Miss Chilcott, also a little pale by this time.

"Oh, Miss Chilcott, don't expel me—oh, don't expel me too!"

"Expel you—*too?*" said Miss Chilcott, very slowly. "Was the letter—were both the letters—to Anita Lyon?"

Winifred sobbed wildly, but she gave some sort of miserable nod that seemed to mean assent.

Miss Chilcott sat perfectly stiff and silent. The blow was so unexpected. She had thought to hear of some foolish piece of schoolgirl disobedience, but—not this. Her thoughts were whirling. Could it possibly be Winifred—*Winifred*, the crushed and quiet, rather stupid girl who always seemed to do her limited best in the most meritorious way—who was at the bottom of the trouble vaguely brooding over the school for so long? It seemed incredible.

"I must talk to you about this to-morrow, when I have had time to think it over," said Miss Chilcott, with stiff lips. She rose from her chair; and the next moment Winifred was up in bed again, clutching at her skirt.

"Miss Chilcott, you won't expel me?—you won't expel me?"

"I don't know what I shall do," said Miss Chilcott sternly: and then looked at the poor terrified thing and softened a little. She remembered that Winifred had a stern and hard father of whom she was mortally afraid.

"I don't think you are likely to be expelled, Winifred; but this is a very serious business, you know."

"I know—I know!" Winifred sobbed wildly. "Oh, I am most dreadfully sorry! Oh, do forgive me! Oh, I'll never, *never* do it again!"

"No. I do not think there will be any fear—or chance—of your ever doing it again," said Miss Chilcott. "Now leave off crying—

that will do no good, and you will only make yourself ill. I will send you up something hot, and you need not come down to breakfast in the morning."

In the office, Miss Pember was impatiently waiting. She was, as has been seen, a little apt to make light of Miss Chilcott's over-anxieties, but she took a sufficiently serious view of this one.

"You see—the Anita influence *is* at work in the school," Miss Chilcott represented miserably. "And after so long—nearly two years!"

"Yes. I'm afraid you are right, Amy," said Miss Pember; and she only called Miss Chilcott by her Christian name—although they were friends of so long standing—on the most serious occasions.

"But that it should be Winifred, of all people! The last girl in the school, I really think, that I should have suspected!"

Miss Pember said nothing. She sat staring into the fire, with her chin in her hand.

"She is a weak creature at the best of times," said Miss Chilcott, "but I never thought there was the least harm in her. And she hardly knew Anita! Two years ago, she was only a child in the Second Form."

Miss Pember suddenly moved and spoke sharply. "Don't be too hard on the wretched Winifred. We are not at the bottom of this yet!"

"WELL! what about Winifred?" asked Miss Pember, appearing in the office after breakfast the next morning.

"I've not been up to her yet," said Miss Chilcott. "And I told them not to take her breakfast till half-past eight. There's no object in leaving the poor thing to lie awake and fret longer than is necessary. I hope she is still asleep."

"Not now. It *is* just half-past," said Miss Pember, looking at her little wrist-watch, which was always invariably right. "But—well, I made sure you had had a harassing interview with her! You look like it."

"Do I? My looks have nothing to do with Winifred this morning—or very little," said Miss Chilcott, who certainly was noticeably pale.

"Nothing to do with Winifred!" repeated Miss Pember, staring.

"No. Read this letter."

Miss Pember took it, flicking on her reading-glasses with her quick, jerky motion. She turned immediately to the end.

"Bass!—Ella's people?"

Miss Chilcott nodded, leaning wearily back in her chair. Miss Pember read the letter through with great attention, turning back once or twice to make sure of the last sentence. It was not a long letter.

"Well! So Ella is unhappy here, and they wish to take her away at the end of this term, and they are willing to pay an extra half-term's fee if you exact it! What does that mean, do you suppose?"

"Just what everything else does, I suppose," said Miss Chilcott hopelessly.

"You mean the Anita craze, of course? Well," said Miss Pember briskly, "let's see if there isn't some other possible explanation, before we begin to sit down and weep about that! Ella is not a popular girl, never has been. She hates being called Beer—though I don't know what else she could expect! She has had three returns in the last week, and she loathes Mademoiselle."

"None of those is enough to account for this letter," mourned Miss Chilcott.

"No. I grant you that," Miss Pember agreed. "For Ella isn't a fool, though she is stupid and not very attractive. I imagine the real difficulty is that she has never made any sort of real friend."

"I thought she and Rita seemed very friendly at one time," said Miss Chilcott.

Miss Pember darted a quick glance at her, but said nothing.

"However, of course Rita is much higher in the school and a very different type of girl," said Miss Chilcott. "And after she got into the Sixth Form—yes, Jessie?"

The housemaid who had appeared at the door looked rather odd.

"If you please, ma'am, Miss Ray is not in her room."

"Not in her room!" Miss Chilcott repeated.

"No, ma'am. I took up her breakfast at half-past eight, as you said, and she wasn't there. I put it down and went along the passage to speak to Emma, and when I came back I thought I had better look in again."

"And she was *still* not there?"

"No, ma'am."

"Thank you, Jessie. I will see about it," said Miss Chilcott.

The door closed, and she and Miss Pember looked at each other.

"All her things went down to be dried, didn't they?" said Miss Pember acutely.

"Yes, everything—thick coat and all. They were soaked. I should think they are hardly dry yet."

Miss Pember went quickly out of the room, reappearing two minutes later.

"They are all still in the kitchen, and not dry yet, as you say."

"We must go up and see," said Miss Chilcott, a little breathlessly.

Upstairs there was nothing to see but an empty room and an untouched breakfast tray. Miss Chilcott gave a quick glance out of the window. It was still raining hard.

"She can't have—"

Miss Pember was rummaging briskly through drawers and hanging cupboard.

"Of course there would have been no difficulty about under-things. Her Sunday frock is not here, or her Sunday hat."

"But she couldn't have gone without a coat—"

"She was wearing her blazer yesterday, wasn't she? Yes, I remember seeing it with the other wet things in the kitchen. Well, she could have worn a woollen coat of some sort—she was sure to have one—and her mackintosh. I'll just go down and see if that is in the cloak-room."

She whisked out, while Miss Chilcott stared out of the window into the rain, and whisked back again after an amazingly short interval.

"Yes, it's gone—and so has she!"

"What *is* to be done?" Miss Chilcott almost whispered.

"Well—not set the whole school chattering, if it's possible to avoid it. It's no use to ask if any door was found unlocked this morning; she could have got out in half a dozen different ways. What an enormous pity that she had a room to herself!—but it's no use thinking of that now. May I have the car?"

"Yes, of course. Where are you going?"

"To the station," said Miss Pember crisply, and whisked out of the room to her own, only pausing for a moment to say:

"For goodness' sake, carry on as well as you can while I'm gone! I'll be as quick as possible."

How Miss Chilcott "carried on," she would never afterwards have been able to say. It seemed to her half a lifetime before she heard the car in the avenue again, and hurried away from the class that she was taking.

"I won't be a minute, girls. Look over the next part till I come back."

Had she had any faint hope that Miss Pember, in her wonderful executive way, would have succeeded in finding the truant and bringing her back? If so, it died a very quick death, for Miss Pember was alone.

"Yes. She went off all right, by the workman's train at half-past six from the Junction. I got them to telegraph through."

"The Junction—ten miles away!" gasped Miss Chilcott. "How in the world did she get there?"

"Walked, I suppose," said Miss Pember. "She would not be likely to get any sort of lift between four and five in the morning."

"But—it must have been pitch dark!" Miss Chilcott cried in horror.

"Pitch dark; and I understand that it has never stopped raining all night."

"And Winifred is a delicate girl—"

"And a timid girl, too. She must have had some very strong reason for doing a thing like this," said Miss Pember.

There was a very brief pause.

"Well—shall I go and telegraph to her people?"

"I—suppose you must," said Miss Chilcott, with dry white lips.

"Just find the address for me, will you? I don't know it."

Miss Chilcott opened a drawer, and turned over an address-book with shaking hands, finally pointing out a page. She seemed quite unable to say another word.

"London—well, that's a blessing, anyhow," said Miss Pember, jotting it down. "She may have gone straight home. What are her people like?"

"A little crushed mother, rather like Winifred herself," Miss Chilcott answered faintly, after trying twice to speak without success. "And a stern tyrant of a father, who settles everything without reference to anybody."

"Wh—ew!" said Miss Pember, and pulled on her gloves, preparatory to starting off again through the rain.

"Please, ma'am, a telegram."

"*You* open it!" Miss Chilcott motioned feebly to Miss Pember, who briskly did so.

"It's all right. No answer," she called briskly to the waiting maid. "Cheer up, Amy, she's safe."

"At—her home?"

"Yes. This is evidently from the tyrant father," said Miss Pember and read aloud:

"'Winifred arrived here 7.55: returning by car this afternoon.'"

"Thank Heaven!" said Miss Chilcott.

"Poor Winifred!" said Miss Pember.

It had been known long before this, of course, all through the school, that Winifred Ray had run away. The buzz and clack was something beyond expression, the amount of work that was done was infinitesimal. Miss Pember made short work of the whole business. She collected the whole school in the hall, and briefly addressed them.

"You know, of course, that Winifred Ray got into trouble last night for going out to post a letter, and this morning she was not to be found. She is safe at her home. She is coming back this afternoon. Now there is the whole truth for you. Please don't imagine all sorts of things for which there is no foundation!"

The whole school stood breathless.

"I don't know," said Miss Pember, "what her reason was for this extraordinary conduct—probably we shall find that out when she returns. Perhaps some of *you* know more about it than I do!"

She ran her sharp eye along the ranks of listening girls, and if it lingered on one more than another, Rita was that one. But there was nothing to be learned from her as she stood calm, collected, perfectly at her ease.

"Go back to your class-rooms," said Miss Pember, "and do try to behave like rational creatures and not like a set of hysterical monkeys!"

In the afternoon, through the pouring rain, Winifred returned, a white and terrified girl, escorted by a stern and terrible father. Miss Chilcott's interview with him, though brief, was the most unpleasant that she had ever had with any parent.

"I don't know," he told her sharply, "what is the cause of this most extraordinary incident. Do you?"

"I am sorry. I have no idea," said Miss Chilcott.

"Then I recommend you to find out, without loss of time," said Mr. Ray. "I can get nothing out of Winifred, but I never expected to. All girls are fools."

His tone and manner said sufficiently plainly that he put schoolmistresses in much the same class.

"I have brought her back as a matter of discipline, of course, and you must deal with her as you think fit. But I wish to remove her at the end of the term."

"Certainly, if you wish," said Miss Chilcott, doing her best to behave with dignity in a very trying position.

"A school in which this sort of incident occurs and where no one knows the reason why," said Mr. Ray, "is no fit school for any girl, in my opinion; and I shall not trouble to hide what I think from other people, if they ask me. Good afternoon."

He went noisily away through the hall to his car, chugging away noisily outside. And Miss Chilcott said to Miss Pember:

"What in the world are we to do?"

"Go up and speak to Winifred," Miss Pember advised sensibly. "I don't wonder that she wouldn't make any sort of confession or disclosure to a man like that! But don't be *too* gentle with her, Amy."

There was, however, nothing at all to be extracted from Winifred, even when she had been comforted with tea and assured that she was not going to be expelled. She was sorry—dreadfully, *dreadfully* sorry! She would never, never, never do such a thing again.

"You will not have the chance here, Winifred," Miss Chilcott told her sorrowfully. "Your father says that he wishes you to leave at the end of the term."

She was watching the girl as she spoke; and it seemed the very last injury to see an obvious relief flash into her face.

"You don't wish to stay, I am afraid?"

"Oh, Miss Chilcott, I—"

"Winifred, I do try my best to make my girls happy. Won't you tell me what is the matter?"

But Winifred couldn't or wouldn't. She sobbed out that she loved Miss Chilcott, she loved the school, she had been happy—and yet there was no doubt at all that she wanted most badly to go away. It was hurtfully evident that, even now that she no longer feared expulsion and knew that she was not going to be punished—"for you have punished yourself quite enough," said Miss Chilcott—she would have been eagerly glad to leave for good that very day.

"Of course!" said Miss Pember, when sorrowfully informed of this. "I could have told you so, without any talking to Winifred."

"But *why?*"

"Ah! that is what we have got to find out—and pretty quickly too, or we shall have no school left to find out about," said Miss Pember.

"I am not going to punish her. She has punished herself enough already," said Miss Chilcott, repeating what she had already said to the culprit upstairs. "I can't bear to think what that poor nervous girl must have suffered, running along in the dark and the rain this morning. I shall not be at all surprised if she is seriously ill."

"No," said Miss Pember; and stopped short very suddenly, as if she had been going to say more and had thought better of it.

"What else were you going to say?" Miss Chilcott asked apprehensively. "You don't think I *ought* to have punished her, do you?"

"No—oh, no!" said Miss Pember, in her driest tone. "She has been punished enough—far too much, as a matter of fact. Besides—"

"Besides what?"

"*You* won't punish her," said Miss Pember. "But I shall be very much mistaken if someone else doesn't."

"What *do* you mean?"

"Ah!" said Miss Pember. "If I could tell you that, I could tell you what is wrong with the school."

CHAPTER XIV

Silhouettes

DOROTHY was feeling thoroughly upset and uncomfortable, and for this there were several reasons.

In the first place, she had lost a page of the story that she was writing; but that was not very important. She could write it again without much difficulty, though it was annoying and a waste of time to have to do so.

In the second place—much more important—there was the unforgettable feeling of the F.G. pervading everything. She didn't, of course, count herself a member any longer, whatever Rita might say. When the usual notice appeared with its usual mystery on the Notice Board, disappearing again in the same rapid, mysterious manner, she took no steps about it. She didn't keep her tryst outside the cloak-room on the Tuesday, and she had no means of knowing, therefore, if Rita did. But she kept on realising most uncomfortably that all the other members would have obeyed the summons, and that there must have been some reason for it, and that therefore something unknown was probably brewing among the chosen few.

In the third place, and most important of all, there was a feeling of responsibility which grew out of this. She *knew* that Blanche was a member of the Society, and she saw quite clearly that Blanche was miserable. She knew that Ada Ling belonged; and, though Ada was much older and therefore had more self-control, she didn't look happy either. Dorothy's actual knowledge stopped there, of course, but she had a very shrewd suspicion that the terrible Winifred business derived from the same source. It had been strictly forbidden in the school to ask Winifred any questions, or to refer to the matter in any way, but she was known to be leaving at the end of the term and that spoke for itself. So, too, was Ella Bass; and though there was in her case no embargo upon questions, she gave very little satisfaction. Did she want to go? Yes, she did! She would be jolly glad to see the last of St. Madern's and everybody in it. Beyond that sweeping statement, she shut a sullen mouth and said nothing, and as nobody cared particularly about her, the subject was soon dropped.

But Dorothy considered the matter very anxiously indeed; for as has been said, she felt responsible. It was not to be denied that Miss Chilcott looked sad and depressed, and of course, she must hate to be losing girls like this for no acknowledged reason. And Dorothy had not forgotten what her mother had said about her head mistress, and what she herself had promised. This did seem to be exactly the occasion for strenuous backing up, but—how was it to be done? If she had definitely known any guilty secrets connected with the F.G., of course her duty would have been plain, though exceedingly unpleasant, but she didn't—for you couldn't call a midnight feast a really serious business. She hadn't the faintest idea why Blanche had made that absurd excursion into the rain, and she had no real reason for connecting it with the F.G., whatever she might suspect. In the same way, the Winifred business told her nothing. It had leaked out, of course, that there had been something about posting a clandestine letter, and that was, according to the St. Madern's code, a pretty grave offence. It was quite enough to make a timorous creature like Winifred try to run away from the consequences of it, though she must indeed have been terribly frightened to slip off like that in the wet darkness of an early winter morning. Could it be possible to find out in any way something that might be of some slight help to Miss Chilcott?

Dorothy tackled Ella first, and, after a very disagreeable interview, retired baffled. Ella sulkily repeated just what she had said to everybody else—she was glad to be leaving and there was nothing at St. Madern's that she would be sorry to leave behind. Anyhow, she wasn't going to be badgered and pumped by *anybody*—Dorothy, or Hester Pyke, or any other prying person. And at that moment Rita came walking in upon them and the discussion dropped perforce, leaving Dorothy rather hot about the cheeks. How hateful to be compared with Hester, the Paul Pry of the school! And how hard, when she didn't personally care a straw about Ella and her doings in any way; she was only trying to be of some use to Miss Chilcott.

With Winifred, her attempt was less unpleasant but quite as fruitless. She was a good deal handicapped by that definite prohibition about referring in any way to the posting escapade and subsequent flight; but it was easy, of course, to say quite sincerely that she was sorry Winifred was leaving.

"So am I—for lots of things," Winifred agreed, looking pensive.

"St. Madern's is so jolly! I can't see why anyone should want to leave for *any* reason," Dorothy probed further.

"Can't you? No, I suppose *you* can't," said Winifred with a queer side-glance.

"I? Why *I* more than anyone else?"

Winifred hesitated a little and then burst out.

"Oh, if only I were as brave as you, Dorothy! If I'd done—what you did—I shouldn't be leaving now, and there wouldn't have been any trouble. If *only* I had!"

"Can't you do it now?" Dorothy persisted eagerly.

"No, I can't. It's too late—and I'm afraid to. It can't be helped; but oh, how I wish—"

Her voice trailed away weakly and her eyes had wandered in a scared fashion towards the door. Dorothy, looking that way too, saw Rita standing there.

"Come along, you two," she said, in a perfectly even voice. "It's such a hopeless day again, that Miss Pember has promised to make silhouettes. I believe she does them most awfully well."

"What are silhouettes?" Winifred asked, in a scared voice.

"Oh, you know! Those black outline pictures, that one sees in shops sometimes," said Dorothy. "Mother has the funniest old picture of all her family—her grandfather and grandmother and her mother and uncles and aunts. And she had one done of me once in London, when I was quite small."

"How are they done?"

"I can't remember exactly, it was so long ago. But we shall soon see."

Miss Pember, in her business-like way, had everything ready, paper that was black on one side and white on the other, pencil, scissors, little hand-lamp to throw a strong shadow. Also, in her business-like way, she lost no time about the matter.

"Sixth Form first—good gracious, only four of you!" she said. "However, Phyllis and Kitty would make anything but a pretty silhouette in their present condition. Sit there, Rita, and keep quite still. Yes, thanks, that's all. Now, Gwen, you next. Celia, be ready when I want you. You Fifth Form people, I shall be ready for you in five minutes, so don't go away."

Her energetic pencil went rapidly round one outline after another.

"I'll cut them all out together presently," she said. "It only wastes time now. Winifred, keep *still!* You don't want to come out with a nose like a lump of putty, do you? No, *please* don't apologise, or I can't do your mouth at all!"

It was amusing to watch at first, and then rather dull. Miss Pember saw instantly when people were beginning to get bored.

"Only one more after this; and then I'll start cutting out," she said; and in two minutes her sharp scissors were snipping cleverly round the outline on the white side of the paper. Then it was turned over, and lo! lying on a white table-cloth, there was the cleverest silhouette of one after another. The girls were rapturous, comparing and exclaiming, though most people discovered with disappointment that their noses were quite a different shape from what they had always supposed.

"They *are* good, Miss Pember! But Rita's is the best."

Yes, Rita's was the best, by common consent. Her rather beaky nose and heavy eyebrows came out most unmistakably.

"You *are* clever, Miss Pember! Thank you most awfully!"

"Clever—rubbish!" said Miss Pember. "Any one of you could do it just as well, with a little practice. And now I've something else to do and you have my leave to depart!"

"Well," she said briskly to Miss Chilcott, who had been an amused spectator of all this, "that disposes of one wet afternoon at least! And I trust it's given a little turn to their thoughts—which isn't a difficult matter with girls! They were all getting mopish and nervy. Dear me, what a long time it is since I played this game before!"

She was vigorously rummaging in a drawer.

"Yes, here are the old ones—and how one forgets girls, after a couple of years!"

"*I* don't," said Miss Chilcott.

"Don't you? Well, if you can put a name to all these old silhouettes, I—I'll put half a crown in the missionary box!"

"I *never* forget my old girls," said Miss Chilcott, a little piqued.

"Here you are then—but no looking for the name on the back, please!" said Miss Pember, handing over a neat pile of silhouettes. "Or look here—I'll make it a little more difficult for you, by mixing to-day's lot with the old ones!"

"Very well," said Miss Chilcott, accepting the challenge with a smile. Perhaps she too was very willing to pass away the wet afternoon with something new, and to forget if possible the shadow that brooded over the school.

She took the silhouettes and laid them aside, one by one, naming each.

"Irene Brown—that is a very good one. Sylvia Pell. Winifred Ray. Hester Pyke. Juliet Merridew—yes, she really is hard to recognise, but then she had such a very little nose. Dorothy Grayling. Celia Tanner—what a pretty delicate profile she had! Helen Cox. Edith Peters. Rita Salmon."

Miss Pember stretched out a quick hand, and then drew it back again as quickly. If Miss Chilcott had not been intent upon the silhouettes, she would have been astonished at the extraordinary expression on the little dark face beside her.

"That's enough—you shall see me put the half-crown in at tea-time, for you've earned it admirably," said Miss Pember. "No, I can't let you look at any more now: some other time if you like, but just now I can't waste another minute. There's something to do at once that I had never thought of."

She began hastily stacking away her pictures in the drawer again; and Miss Chilcott discovered with surprise that it was very much later than she had thought, and that she also must go and get busy without loss of time. As she shut the door behind her, Miss Pember's quick hands fell into her lap; she was staring intently at one of the silhouettes that lay before her.

"I never thought of it—but of course eyes and hair make all the difference," she said half aloud. "Well—one more nail in that young woman's coffin, if I am not very much mistaken. But—happy thought! I'll go and submit them to Nannie!"

Nannie was the school nurse, not a trained nurse, but a very wise woman who knew most things that there are to know about girls, and had no difficulty in deciding whose headache was really bad and needed a morning in bed, and whose headache was just malingering because of an unlearnt French lesson. She knew also the difference between the ordinary snuffle-cold and the cold that means measles; and she knew—a much more difficult matter—when tears needed sympathy and when they needed snubbing. She had once been Miss Chilcott's own nurse, in days unimaginably far back, and she had come with her to St. Madern's, and proved herself quite invaluable, and considered the school—and Miss Chilcott too, for that matter—very much as her own family.

"I've been doing some more silhouettes, Nannie, because everyone was so bored this wet afternoon and I thought you'd like to see them," said Miss Pember, coming briskly into her cosy little room.

Nannie was delighted, and full of praise: only a little critical of Celia's, which she thought hardly good-looking enough. But then Celia was, as everyone knew, her special pet in the school, because she was delicate and always ailing, and had given more trouble in that way than all the other girls put together.

"Do you know this one?" said Miss Pember.

Did Nannie know it! She was quite offended at the question. Why, it was Miss Purcell, of course, with her hair all anyhow as usual.

"How do you like this?" asked Miss Pember.

Nannie stiffened a little, saying in a rather snorty voice that it was very good indeed; she would have known Miss Salmon anywhere.

"But you don't quite like it, do you? Do you think it doesn't do *her* justice?" Miss Pember inquired slily.

"It does her all the justice she wants, Miss Pember," said Nannie, and laid the silhouette aside with decided fingers.

"Poor Rita!" said Miss Pember, laughing and taking it up, "I really believe you are prejudiced against her, Nannie, because she is never ill—except with this mumps, and that she couldn't help—and never gives you any trouble."

"I've nothing *against* Miss Salmon," said Nannie, in her stiffest possible tone; and both that and her manner said most emphatically that she had nothing *for* Rita, either.

"Well—that's the last of them," said Miss Pember, gathering them up. "And now I must go. It's very nearly tea-time."

"Thank you very much, Miss Pember," said Nannie.

"I thought you'd like to see them," said Miss Pember, and whisked out of the room in her sudden way, as if she were in a great hurry.

But outside in the passage she stopped suddenly, turning over again the silhouette that lay on the top of her pile. It had a name written on the back: but the name was not Rita's.

CHAPTER XV

ADA IN THE NIGHT

IF only Caroline did not snore so! Dorothy reflected crossly, waking from a sound sleep. She was noted, of course, for this unpopular accomplishment, and it was aggravated by the fact that, once she was fairly off, you might have fired a pistol at her ear without waking her until she had had her sleep out. People who slept in the same room had to get used to it or lie awake, and being schoolgirls they got used to it. But to-night it must have been some really portentous snort that roused Dorothy with such a jump.

She listened crossly, and there was no sound of snoring at all.

Well, so much to the good! Caroline must have half-roused even herself—she did, sometimes—and have turned over and gone off again more peacefully. It would be well to take advantage of this, before the snoring began again. Dorothy turned round and tucked the bedclothes more tightly in at her back. It was a very cold night.

The next moment she turned over quickly and listened hard; for there the sound was again, and it hadn't been Caroline at all—nor had it been snoring. It was a moaning, unearthly voice saying words that were perfectly distinct.

"No, Rita! I can't—I won't! Please, please don't ask me!"

An unexpected voice in the night always has an eerie effect: when it is the voice of a person talking in her sleep, it is creepy in the extreme. Dorothy felt herself go quite cold. She had a momentary wonder whether her hair was standing on end, like the hair of frightened people in books.

"All right—I'm coming, I'm coming!" the voice went on; and there was a sudden sound of movement. There was a slipping out of bed, a shuffling sound as of feet hunting for slippers.

Dorothy sat upright in her bed. What in the world was she to do? For the first time since coming to St. Madern's, she wished that

Caroline did not sleep so heavily, for a second person to share the responsibility would have been an amazing comfort. But Caroline slept on, softly snoring and quite impervious to sounds of any sort.

There was a little creaking of the floor; someone—Ada, of course—was moving about in her cubicle. What on earth was she going to do?

"Yes, Rita, I'll post the letter—I really will. Only don't ask me again—promise that you won't!"

The cubicle curtain was being pulled back Dorothy jumped out of bed and felt for her slippers and dressing-gown in a hurry. Her heart was beating fast, and she was frightened. You mustn't wake a sleep-walker suddenly, she knew that. You must just follow, and take any opportunity that offers of making her come back with you.

Ada was opening the door—not as one opens a door in the night, secretly and with caution, but in ordinary daytime fashion. Would anyone hear and come? But they were at the end of a corridor, and there was no other room near but Rita's, and Dorothy devoutly hoped that she *wouldn't* come.

There was always a certain amount of light left burning in the passages all night long, and Ada walked out with the calm assurance of a person doing a perfectly usual thing at a perfectly usual time— she *couldn't* be asleep. But she turned her head for a moment, as if listening to something, and Dorothy saw that she most certainly was, with eyes tight shut. It was the creepiest thing possible.

She walked, and Dorothy walked after her, straight down the corridor and down the stairs; and there Dorothy held her breath with terror, for it seemed as if she *must* fall, with her eyes tight shut like that. But no. Down she went, with the most perfect success, and down another flight and into the hall and towards the front door. It seemed amazing to Dorothy that no one heard; but after all, two girls in bedroom slippers make very little sound on carpeted stairs—for it was the front stairs by which Ada had come down. But now there must be a noise, for she was putting her hand on the door and it was, of course, locked and bolted and chained. If she tried to undo all those fastenings, there would be the most frightful clash and clatter—

She turned the handle; and, of course, nothing happened. She turned it again; and her face, hitherto perfectly calm and peaceful, grew disturbed.

"I can't undo it, Rita! *Rita!*" she said, in a loud whisper.

Dorothy put a very gentle hand on her shoulder, thinking madly of all she had ever heard about the proper way to treat people who walked in their sleep. One mustn't frighten them—but sometimes they would answer if they were spoken to, without waking up.

"You can't open it. It's locked," she whispered back. "Come back to bed, Ada."

"But I haven't posted the letter," Ada answered her, quite reasonably, in that odd unnatural voice.

"There is no letter to post. You have made a mistake," said Dorothy breathlessly.

She slipped her hand—a very cold one—into Ada's, which was quite comfortably warm; and Ada, who was always a quiet, tractable creature, responded with a merciful willingness. Through the hall again—up the stairs—up the second flight—along the corridor—

They were nearly at their own door again, when another door opened suddenly without a sound—Rita's. And there stood Rita herself in the doorway, new blue dressing-gown: and black pigtail and all.

"What does this mean?" she asked, in an almost soundless voice.

"Hush—hush!" Dorothy motioned to her wildly; for Ada seemed to have heard that voice through her sleep, and paused and looked distressed.

"Put her to bed, then, and I will speak to you to-morrow," said Rita softly, and closed her door again without a sound. And, as it closed, Ada woke up.

"Where am I?—What on earth has happened? *Was that Rita?*"

She turned white as she asked the last question, in quite a different tone from her first words.

"It's all right—do get into bed again as fast as you can!" Dorothy whispered frantically; and hurried her through their own door and shut it after them.

"Dorothy! Dorothy! Such awful dreams!"

"Hush, old girl! See, I'll help you off with your dressing-gown. … Don't bother about your shoes. I'll take them off after you're in bed. …"

"Such dreams! such dreams!" Ada kept sobbing and crying, as she clung to Dorothy.

"What sort of dreams?"

"Oh, *horrible!* All about secret societies, and the dreadful things that were done to anyone who betrayed them—"

Ada shivered and shook under the clothes that Dorothy was pulling around her.

"Who told you all that sort of thing?"

Ada opened her mouth to speak, and then shut it again in a hurry.

"You needn't tell me. I know!" said Dorothy furiously.

"Oh, please, Dorothy, you *don't* know—I didn't tell you anything!" Ada cried out wildly, half starting up.

"No, you didn't. Don't worry," said Dorothy.

"But you won't—you won't say that I—"

"Of course I won't. You haven't mentioned any name at all," said Dorothy, who was really frightened by the terror of the poor shaking thing, and anxious to soothe her by any means in her power. "Now, go to sleep as fast as you can. Do you know what time it is?"

"I'm afraid to go to sleep. I'm afraid of dreaming again, and walking again," Ada moaned.

"You shan't do that—*I'll* see to it," Dorothy promised firmly. "See, can you make room for me in your bed? I think we can manage, and then you needn't be afraid of anything!"

"Oh, yes, I am sure we can manage—if you won't be too uncomfortable," Ada promised eagerly, screwing herself into the smallest possible space. And, clinging to Dorothy's hand, she very soon fell asleep and slept quietly.

But Dorothy lay awake—yes, until the clock had struck two and even three, raging with indignation. What a wicked, cruel shame to have deliberately frightened a naturally nervous girl like that! Rita would speak to her next day, would she? Very well! But two people could speak, if it came to that, and Dorothy would have one or two things to say to Rita on her own part. …

It is not too easy in a school—especially in the winter, when there is no possibility of finding a quiet garden corner—to have a private conversation with anyone. Breakfast and prayers and lessons and walk and dinner came, with never a chance of getting Rita to herself and telling her a few home-truths. In the afternoon there was hockey, and Dorothy had her massage and lay down for her appointed time; and as she lay she did not read or write, but went over and over again her causes of complaint, while her indignation waxed hotter and hotter. By tea-time it was at a very fine temperature indeed; and after tea the desired opportunity came at last.

"Rita, can I speak to you, please?"

It required a great effort to say that calmly and inoffensively, feeling as Dorothy felt. Rita appeared to notice nothing wrong, for she answered with perfect coolness.

"Yes, certainly. I wanted to see you too, you know. What about the passage outside the cloakroom?"

It was the last place that Dorothy herself would have chosen, filled as it was with unpleasant F.G. associations. But she put up her chin and returned Rita's cool stare defiantly. ... If only she wasn't so intensely calm and unruffled! It is difficult to say necessary furious things to a person who looks at you like that.

"By the way, Dorothy, why were you out of your room last night?"

Dorothy stared for a minute without answering. She was too much taken aback to speak.

"Why, you know, Rita! Ada was walking in her sleep."

"Yes. So you say," Rita returned, with all imaginable coolness. "She was certainly awake when I spoke to you."

"It was your speaking that woke her!"

"Yes. So you say," Rita repeated calmly. "All I can answer for is, that you two were walking about the house in the middle of the night."

Rage choked Dorothy so that for a moment she stammered and could not speak.

"It's rather a serious offence, you know. By rights, I ought to report you," said Rita.

"You—you—you *know* that Ada was walking in her sleep! And you know what made her do it!" Dorothy exclaimed.

"Do I? I wasn't aware of it," said Rita, with raised eyebrows.

"If there is any reporting to be done, it's I and not you who ought to do it!" Dorothy gasped. "It's a shame—a wicked, cruel *shame!*—to frighten her so that she had bad dreams and walks in them!"

"Don't I remember that that was what you did yourself, once upon a time?" Rita retorted coolly.

Dorothy was pretty red already; but she turned a little more so, from a different cause.

"I *did* frighten Ada with a story told in bed; but that was just after I came, when I had no idea that that sort of thing was bad for her," she defended herself. "And I was most frightfully sorry about it and confessed to Miss Chilcott at once—you *know* I did!"

Rita said nothing, but her smile was maddening.

"But *you*—you knew that she was easily frightened and how bad it was for her!" Dorothy choked out furiously "and you told her frightening things on purpose—"

"Did she tell you so?"

"No. She didn't," said Dorothy, suddenly alive to the fact that she might be getting Ada into fresh trouble instead of helping her. "But she told me what her dreams had been about, and I *know* that it was you who did it."

"You seem to know a great deal; almost too much, perhaps," said Rita.

The sneering malice of the tone drove Dorothy beyond all limits of prudence.

"Yes, I do know—and Miss Chilcott shall know too!" she exclaimed. "I would go and tell her now, at once, if she hadn't got people to tea. But I shall tell her the first thing to-morrow—and I don't care *what* you do!"

"I'm afraid I was mistaken in you," said Rita. "I did think, Dorothy, that you were the sort of girl who believed in keeping promises, and that when you said you would keep a secret, you might be relied upon to keep it."

The calm comment brought Dorothy up with a round turn, for she *was* that kind of girl.

"What do you mean?" she cried.

"You know quite well what I mean," said Rita.

And here Dorothy found herself up against one of the most difficult problems of right and wrong. For a promise should undoubtedly be held sacred; and yet what about those promises given, as hers had been, under a perfectly wrong impression? A Secret Society had been, from her point of view, just a rather elaborate form of amusement for a few chosen girls: not at all a thing that was injuring the school and making people ill and miserable.

"I should never have joined if I had known the sort of thing you did!" she cried.

"But you *did* join," Rita persisted calmly.

And that was true; and, if she went to Miss Chilcott with the tale of the F.G., she would undoubtedly be breaking her word. It was unpleasant in the extreme.

As she paused, considering this with a much disturbed mind, Rita made her first false move.

"Besides—I don't quite see *what* you are going to tell," she said.

But Dorothy saw, quite plainly and in a sudden comforting flash. It was not until the question was plainly put to her like that, that she saw where she stood.

"I promised not to tell about the F.G.," she said, "and, though I'm not quite sure that I ought to keep that promise now that I know such a lot more about it, I don't think I need break it. There's plenty to tell without that!"

"What—for instance?" asked Rita, in a queer, breathless voice.

Dorothy knew pretty well that she stood on very dangerous ground. She paused to think over her reply before she made it.

"There's no promise to keep me from telling about Ada last night," she said. "About her walking in her sleep because she was frightened out of her life, and the sort of thing that had frightened her. I don't *know* who did it, but I daresay Miss Chilcott can find out!"

There was a little pause; the sort of pause that detective-stories describe as "tense."

"Well? Is that all?" Rita drawled dangerously.

"No. It isn't all," said Dorothy, her brain working quicker and quicker with the stimulus of danger. "While she was walking in her sleep, she was talking too, and it was all about posting a letter for you!"

The pause this time was a little longer.

"Well?" said Rita.

The most brilliant flash of all came to Dorothy.

"I promised not to tell about the F.G.," she said. "But I never promised not to tell about you—*you*, a girl in the Sixth!—giving a midnight feast!"

"That was part of the F.G.," Rita struck in swiftly. And a more experienced person than Dorothy might have noticed that it was the first time she had attempted to defend herself: a very dangerous sign.

"No, it wasn't," Dorothy retorted. "I promised to join a Secret Society, but I should *never* have promised to join in doing that sort of thing, dead against the rules."

If you are having a difference of opinion with a wild cat—always an inadvisable thing to do—it is extremely rash to drive it into a position where it cannot turn either way: it is practically certain to spring at you. That Rita did not spring, either literally or figuratively, shows the difference between a wild cat and a very dangerous girl.

Her black eyes had gone curiously dull. She stood looking at Dorothy for quite a minute, in the most uncomfortable fashion.

"Well—we shall be late for prep.," was all she said, in a perfectly unruffled voice; and she turned and walked calmly away.

There was nothing for Dorothy to do but to follow her; and this she did, with her head whirling and a feeling of victory dashed with doubt. Why had Rita given in like that so tamely? It was not like her. Was this the end of the game?

"COULD I speak to you, Miss Chilcott?"

"It's very late, Rita," said Miss Chilcott, surprised and disapproving; and so it was—bedtime, in fact.

"You had visitors to tea," Rita represented smoothly.

"Well, what you have to say will keep till to-morrow, surely?"

"It *ought* not to, Miss Chilcott," said Rita, in virtuous accents.

"Oh, well! If it's something that I *ought* to hear—" said Miss Chilcott, as she could not very well help saying. "Come into the office. But be as quick as you can. I am tired."

The office door closed behind them.

"Now then, Rita!"

Miss Chilcott remained standing, and her tone did not indicate a lengthy chat.

"Please, Miss Chilcott, it's about Dorothy Grayling."

"Dorothy Grayling! Is she ill?"

"Oh, *no*, Miss Chilcott! Nothing of that sort."

"What then, Rita?"

Miss Chilcott's tone was attentive now and very much surprised. Whatever she had been expecting, it was very evidently not this.

"Well, Miss Chilcott, last night—*very* late, after midnight—I woke up, thinking I heard a noise. I looked out, and Dorothy was coming along the passage with Ada Ling, from the front staircase."

"Dorothy and Ada! What in the world were they doing?"

"I don't know, Miss Chilcott," said Rita, modestly.

"Had Ada been walking in her sleep again?"

"She *might* have been, Miss Chilcott. She was awake when she passed my door."

"Did you speak to them?"

"I asked them what they were doing, of course, but Dorothy only begged me to say nothing—which of course I *couldn't* do," said Rita, very virtuously indeed. "They went into their room and shut the door, and I heard them talking afterwards—oh, for a long time!"

"Very odd!" said Miss Chilcott, frowning.

"Yes, Miss Chilcott. So I thought," Rita agreed deferentially.

"I must speak to Dorothy about it to-morrow. You were quite right to tell me, of course."

"Thank you, Miss Chilcott."

"Well, good night, Rita."

"Please, Miss Chilcott—that isn't all."

"Not all?" said Miss Chilcott, frowning again.

"I didn't want to worry you unless it was absolutely necessary; and I know you like Dorothy." Rita paused, more modestly than ever.

"I hope I like all my girls," said Miss Chilcott sharply. "Go on!"

"But I *have* found Dorothy—more than once—in other girls' rooms."

"In other girls' rooms?"

"Yes. I can only be *sure* of twice," said Rita painstakingly. "Once, soon after she came, in—in one of the big girls' rooms. I don't want to mention names more than I must, Miss Chilcott—"

"Go on!"

"But she was very new then, she might have forgotten the rule—"

"And the other time?"

"In Blanche Bates' room, the night that she went out and got so wet."

"Oh—there is nothing in *that!*" said Miss Chilcott, with distinct relief in her tone. "I sent her up myself, to see the child out of her wet clothes and into bed."

"Yes, Miss Chilcott, I know. But it was afterwards—the same evening. Dorothy was going into the room in a great hurry, with a box or parcel of some sort."

"A box or parcel?"

"I didn't bother to notice very particularly, I'm afraid," Rita apologised. "I supposed you had sent her up with something."

She paused questioningly, but Miss Chilcott did not answer.

"It was only afterwards—when Blanche was so sick in the night—

that I thought of it again. It made me wonder a little, because of course Dorothy knows her at home and she seems to be fond of her—"

Rita made an effective pause.

"I must inquire into this too," said Miss Chilcott, and her voice was certainly disquieted. "But I daresay—I am sure—there is some quite ordinary explanation."

"Yes, Miss Chilcott. I hope so."

Even now, Rita did not show any signs of going to bed, but stood her ground with a modest persistence.

"Anything more?" Miss Chilcott quite snapped at her.

"Well, yes, Miss Chilcott. But I really do hate to worry you like this—"

"Sit down, and please get on with it as fast as you can," said Miss Chilcott. She sat down herself, in an uncomfortable chair, very upright and attentive.

"You remember the night that you were away at Cambridge?"

"Yes!"

"I—I happen to know that Dorothy that night was at a—a sort of feast—in the bath-room on her landing."

"A sort of feast!"

"It was *very* wrong, I know: especially with you away. That made it seem—as well as breaking such a strict rule—so—so *mean*," said Rita, in a regretful tone of disapproval.

"You should have reported this to me at once, Rita!"

"One doesn't always hear of that sort of thing at once," Rita murmured. "And—and I do hate telling tales. But I *know* that Dorothy was there."

"Do you mean that the feast was of her giving?"

"Oh, Miss Chilcott, I didn't say that, did I? I don't think I ought to. Suppose I had made a mistake about it! But I *do* know that she was there."

Miss Chilcott sat quite still, very stiff and pale. She *did* like Dorothy: she had never had a girl in the school whom she had liked better. And what had Dorothy's mother said to her?

"*I will send you a girl whom you can trust. … Dorothy is entirely and absolutely straight.*"

"What is *that?*" she asked very sharply, for Rita was drawing something from her pocket.

"I—I am afraid you ought to see this," she said, in a reluctant and unhappy voice.

"A *letter?*"

Miss Chilcott's voice expressed the strongest distaste. She felt that she had had enough of letters for the rest of her life.

"I—I'm afraid so," Rita replied, very gravely. "It fell out of her writing-case and I picked it up. Of course I was going to give it back to her at once, but then—I couldn't help seeing what it was, and I thought I ought to bring it to you."

Miss Chilcott took it most reluctantly; but the very first word, as she glanced at it, made her start, and brought quite a new expression into her face, amazed and incredulous.

"It is not signed!" she said sharply.

"No. But it is Dorothy's writing—and her paper. Besides, I picked it up as she dropped it!" Rita replied, as if that assurance left the matter beyond all possibility of doubt.

Miss Chilcott hardly heard. She was reading the letter: a very strange letter, certainly, to be written by a schoolgirl in whom one had had absolute confidence.

"My Dearest Cyril,

"It is very difficult to get letters posted to you, but I hope to manage this somehow, in spite of all prying and over-seeing, which I find almost the worst part of this place. They are quite kind; but I don't know what would happen if this fell into their hands! Of course Mamma would be told; and that would be the end of everything for you and me. Only a little more than a month, darling: and then I hope we shall be able to meet again. I simply live for that—"

The paper was torn there, and Miss Chilcott, reaching that point, sat as if she were stunned. She couldn't believe her own eyes. And yet it was unmistakably Dorothy's writing and the rather odd-coloured paper that she always used. Miss Chilcott had noticed it, with a little amusement, as she looked over the letters before they were posted.

It was so very obviously a rather expensive Christmas present.

She found her voice with difficulty.

"You will leave this with me, Rita, of course. Good night."

Rita rose obediently.

"Good night, Miss Chilcott. I *am* sorry to have had to say all this."

"You cannot be more sorry than I am," said Miss Chilcott.

With her hand on the door, Rita turned once more.

"I forgot just one small thing—I don't know if I ought to mention it—"

"Go on!" said Miss Chilcott, in a dead voice.

"I don't know if you remember—such a silly little thing, but you did ask me, and I didn't know at the time. About a piece of torn paper that you picked up in the hall—"

Miss Chilcott stiffened, and turned a suddenly attentive face.

"It was Dorothy who threw it there, from the top landing," said Rita. "I only found out quite by accident. Little Blanche Bates happened to be passing at the time and she told me. She thought it such a queer thing for anyone to do!"

"Very queer," Miss Chilcott agreed automatically, with stiff lips.

"Of course it wasn't of any importance at all, but you did ask me—"

"*Good night*, Rita!" said Miss Chilcott.

"Good night, Miss Chilcott," said Rita, and faded decorously and deferentially away.

It was a very vain wish as far as Miss Chilcott was concerned, for she lay awake hour after hour, trying to find some means of still believing in Dorothy and finding her hopes grow fainter and fainter as the night wore on. One thing might possibly have been explained away; but so many accusations and all so different—it was a hopeless case. She found herself wishing that the tables had been turned and that Dorothy had been the accuser and Rita the culprit, and then was ashamed of herself—for a head mistress must before all things be just, with no regard for likings or dislikings. What would Miss Pember think? She was clever, but it would take more than her cleverness to draw Dorothy out of this dreadful bog that was closing round her. And how, oh, *how* could Miss Chilcott bring herself to write the terrible letter that would break Dorothy's mother's heart?

Her thoughts went on to the school. A scandal like this—somehow, she instinctively felt that there would be no trusting Rita to keep the details to herself—and another girl expelled would be the end of poor St. Madern's. Yes, the school had been ill-wished by somebody! There was no getting over that, whatever Miss Pember might say: Miss Pember, who had gone to bed early with a bad headache and had not been available to talk over this last final blow Not, Miss Chilcott felt despairingly, that even she could do anything to help here.

She tossed and turned in a restless misery, hearing the big school clock strike one hour after another, while Rita lay peacefully slumbering with a satisfied smile upon her face, like one who feels that she has done her job well and can rest contented.

CHAPTER XVII

"MISS CHILCOTT wants to speak to you, Dorothy," was the message which was given to Dorothy just as she finished breakfast. It was unexpected but very welcome. She couldn't imagine what Miss Chilcott wanted her for, but it was much easier to be summoned than to ask for an interview.

How pale Miss Chilcott looked! Not a bit like herself. Dorothy noticed it and was sorry.

"Sit down, Dorothy."

It wasn't like Miss Chilcott's voice, either, or her manner. Dorothy sat down, beginning to feel slightly uncomfortable. What *could* be coming next?

"Dorothy, I have one or two things to ask you. Will you please give me a perfectly straight answer, Yes or No?"

"Yes, of course, Miss Chilcott!" said Dorothy, rather relieved. For this could surely mean only one thing. Miss Chilcott had heard from some other source the unpleasant things that Dorothy had meant to tell her, and only wanted to have them confirmed. It would simplify matters very much.

"On the night that I was away at Cambridge, is it true that you gave a midnight feast in the bath-room on your landing?"

"*I*—gave a midnight feast?" Dorothy gasped in horror.

Miss Chilcott nodded, looking at her with sad eyes.

"No! No indeed, Miss Chilcott!"

"But there *was* a midnight feast that night?"

"Yes," Dorothy murmured miserably.

"And you were there?"

"Ye—yes, Miss Chilcott."

"Breaking a strict rule of the school? And on a night when I was away, and so you were sure of not being found out?"

Dorothy was growing redder and redder. She burst out.

"Miss Chilcott, I *was* there. But I—I never knew about it beforehand—"

"You never knew about it beforehand! Then why were you in the bath-room at that time of night?"

"I mean—" Dorothy struggled wildly to speak the truth without breaking that hateful promise—"I never knew that it was a feast—or *anything* of that sort. And I never ate anything, or drank anything either."

"You went to a midnight feast, and yet ate and drank nothing!" said Miss Chilcott incredulously; and indeed it did sound a most unlikely statement. "I'm afraid I can hardly believe that, Dorothy."

"It is true—quite true!" Dorothy protested, a lump in her throat thickening her voice. "When I found out what—what it was, I came away at once."

Miss Chilcott only looked at her in silence. It was obvious that she did not believe this very lame tale.

"There is something else," she said, and Dorothy had never had that slow, cold voice from her before. "I picked up a piece of paper in the hall, a torn piece of a letter. I am told that you threw it there—from upstairs, over the banisters."

Dorothy sat silent, clutching her chair on both sides with cold, shaking hands.

"Is that true?"

"Yes, Miss Chilcott."

"Why did you do it?"

Dorothy sat silent again. The only possible answer was, because Rita had told her to, and she could not bring herself to sneak like that.

"Will you please tell me how much you know of Anita Lyon?"

"Of—Anita Lyon?" Dorothy gasped, scarcely believing her ears. What an extraordinary jump from one subject to another which, as far as she knew, was entirely unconnected with it!

"Yes. Please don't tell me that you know nothing of her, for I am afraid I can't believe it."

"I wasn't going to," Dorothy answered, a little indignantly. "When I first came, one of the girls showed me her photograph—in a group, outside my room."

"And is that *all* you know of her?"

"No, Miss Chilcott. I was told that she had been expelled."

"Yes? And what more?"

"*Nothing* more!" Dorothy answered, with determination and a little anger.

"You expect me to believe that—after what you have just owned?"

"I hope you will believe it, Miss Chilcott, for it's true!"

Miss Chilcott gave a quick sigh, very sad and rather impatient.

"Another thing: I am told that you have been found, more than once, in other girls' rooms—breaking another strict rule of the school."

"It isn't true!" Dorothy cried indignantly.

"*Never?*"

Dorothy thought back as far as her fast beating heart would let her.

"The first day I came, one of the—the Sixth Form asked me to go in to her room to be told about something. I'm afraid I *did* forget the rule then—I had only just heard it—"

"One of the Sixth Form—I won't ask you which—deliberately asked you to break a rule which she knew, of course, perfectly well? It doesn't sound very likely, Dorothy."

"It is *true*," Dorothy persisted, scarlet.

"We will leave that. Again—the night that little Blanche Bates went out in the rain—"

"You *said* that it was right of me to have gone up with her to get off her wet clothes!" Dorothy protested wildly.

"Certainly I did. I am not speaking of that. I am told that afterwards—later in the evening—you went back to her room and took her a parcel of some sort."

"It wasn't later, it was directly after," Dorothy defended herself.

"But you *did* take her a parcel?"

"She begged me to bring her attaché-case, which was down in the preparation-room, and I did."

"Her attaché-case," said Miss Chilcott slowly. "Was the Turkish Delight in it, that made her so ill in the night?"

"I don't know what was in it—I didn't look. I don't know anything about any Turkish Delight," said Dorothy.

"It was not that, by any chance, which she had been out in the rain to fetch—for you?"

"*No*, Miss Chilcott!"

It is very difficult to distinguish the scarlet of indignation from the scarlet of guilt; and Dorothy was one of those fair girls who colour extremely for the slightest cause. Miss Chilcott looked at her and looked away again, drawing a paper from her locked desk.

"Is this yours?"

"Yes, Miss Chilcott."

Miss Chilcott's heart—she really liked Dorothy and would have been only too glad to prove her innocent—went down like lead, for this was the last and worst proof. If Dorothy had indignantly denied all acquaintance with that extraordinary letter, Miss Chilcott would only too gladly have done her best to find out that some other girl had written it, stealing paper and imitating handwriting; but now this last hope had gone. Dorothy made no bones about it at all, she owned up at once, without the slightest hesitation—presumably, she knew that denial was useless.

"You wrote it?"

"Yes, Miss Chilcott."

"Did you know that it had dropped out of your writing-case?"

"I—knew that I had lost it," Dorothy stammered. "I couldn't find it anywhere—"

"That must have been rather trying for you!"

Miss Chilcott was very seldom sarcastic, but she had never to deal with a case like this before. It almost seemed as if Dorothy did not realise the enormity of her offence.

"Yes, Miss Chilcott. I had to write it all over again."

Miss Chilcott could hardly believe her ears. She stood up suddenly.

"That will do, Dorothy. Go to your room!

She could not look at the scarlet girl who went silently out—the girl whom she had liked and trusted. Rita had indeed been justified in all her reluctant accusations. Miss Chilcott had been slow to believe in them, had clung to one hope after another until Dorothy herself tore them away by her confessions; but this last barefaced shamelessness—! It was beyond all bounds of possibility.

And—news running through the school with its accustomed wireless rapidity—everyone very speedily knew that Dorothy Grayling was in the most terrible disgrace; that she had done—well, simply everything you could think of! that she was shut up in her room and no one was to go near her; that she would almost certainly be expelled.

"But *what* has she done?"

"Ask Rita. Rita knows all about it!"

"I don't believe it! I don't believe it!" Dorothy's friends and champions (and they were many) clamoured in chorus.

"Well, you just ask Rita, then. *She'll* tell you!"

And Rita did tell: not pouring out her story in full flood as if she enjoyed telling it, but letting it ooze out slowly and with apparent reluctance, by which means she secured its spreading far and wide with the greatest success. She said little and gave a great deal to be understood, so that the accusations against poor Dorothy appeared in a sort of mist of vagueness which swelled them to enormous size. It was not very clearly understood by anybody exactly *what* she had done; but there was something about being in other girls' rooms, and doing mysterious things about the house in the middle of the night, and being in some unknown way implicated with the legendary Anita Lyon, and, worst of all—writing the most awful clandestine letter to some *man*, saying perfectly awful things about the school and even about her own mother! This was, of course, and quite rightly, considered to be beyond the last limit of impossibility.

"She must be a perfect horror!" said St. Madern's, swelling in the proud consciousness of virtue. Of *course* she would be expelled! Why, even the terrible Anita had never done anything remotely resembling these enormous crimes.

Rita, serene amidst the storm, wrote letters and smiled quietly to herself. She refused to say anything more about the matter—there was, indeed, nothing more to be said. She listened to the storm that she had so judiciously raised, well satisfied with her work, and then, having assured herself that it was duly done, she rose and went out of the room.

And, if she had stayed five minutes longer, the fate of

Dorothy Grayling and of St. Madern's in general might have been extraordinarily different.

"*Sorry*, Rita. I didn't know you were coming out!" apologised a rather alarmed small voice. The owner of the voice, who had cannoned into Rita in the doorway, came in with a music-case under her arm and stood surprised at the babble.

"What *is* the matter?" she asked of the nearest girl small enough to be approached by such an insignificant person as herself.

"The matter? Why, haven't you heard?"

"I haven't heard anything. I've been practising."

"Well, it's your precious Dorothy Grayling, that is the matter! Perhaps you won't think quite so much of her now, Blanche Bates!"

"Who— what—?" stammered Blanche, turning pale.

"Why, she's done all sorts of the most awful things, and she'll probably be expelled!"

"She hasn't, she *hasn't!* And she *won't!*"

"She jolly well has. You just listen!" and the speaker, thoroughly enjoying the telling of an oft-told tale to quite a new person, poured out a highly-coloured version of the popular scandal.

"So you see!" she ended.

Blanche, who had listened in perfect silence with a whitening little face, replied briefly and explosively, "She didn't!" and vanished out of the room.

"Where has that child gone?" someone asked, turning as the door banged.

"I don't know," replied her enlightener, and joined a little group to go over the whole thrilling tale once more.

Blanche had gone straight, with a fast-beating heart and the coldest of hands, to Miss Chilcott's office.

"Who is that? Blanche? No, Blanche, I am too busy to see you now," said Miss Chilcott, who was talking to Miss Pember.

But Blanche came in and shut the door behind her.

"I *must* tell you—I *can't* wait!" she gasped.

"Did you not hear what I said, Blanche?" Miss Chilcott returned severely.

"Yes—but I *must* tell you! It's—it's about Dorothy!"

"*What* about Dorothy?" asked Miss Pember, suddenly and sharply.

"She didn't—she didn't do all the dreadful things that they are saying!"

"I am afraid you are mistaken, Blanche. Dorothy has already confessed that she *did*," said Miss Chilcott. "Run away, please."

"Wait a minute," Miss Pember suddenly interposed. "I should like to have one thing confirmed—two things—What about this midnight feast, Blanche?"

Blanche stared with frightened eyes.

"We know that it took place and that Dorothy was there. But we don't know who else—were *you* there, for instance?"

"Ye—yes," Blanche sobbed in a terrified voice.

"Did Dorothy give the party?"

"No—oh, *no!*"

"But she was there?"

"Yes—but she didn't know what it was when she came. She went away at once. She wouldn't eat or drink anything."

Miss Chilcott and Miss Pember exchanged a very quick glance. This part of Dorothy's self-defence had seemed too unlikely to be considered, and yet it now appeared to be true.

"Dorothy went to the bath-room—in the middle of the night—and yet didn't know what she was going to find going on when she got there?" said Miss Pember sharply. "H'm! A very difficult thing to understand!"

Blanche twisted her hands together, looking more frightened than before.

"Now tell us something else, Blanche, since you are here. That night that you ran out in the rain and Dorothy put you to bed—was it she who brought you up that Turkish delight, in your attaché-case?"

"Ye—yes," Blanche murmured faintly.

"She *did* bring it up to you!"

"Ye—yes, Miss Chilcott."

The two mistresses exchanged another glance, of quite a different kind from the last.

"She *said* she did not," said Miss Pember suddenly, in a pouncing manner, which made Blanche jump.

"She—she didn't know it was there, Miss Pember!"

"Didn't know it was there?"

"No. I—I asked her to bring up my case and she did. I didn't tell her what was in it, and she didn't know."

"O—oh!" said Miss Chilcott and Miss Pember together. It was the latter who added quickly:

"So it wasn't Dorothy who gave it to you in the first place?"

"Oh, *no*, Miss Pember!"

Blanche looked most terribly afraid that this prosecution would be carried on into finding out who had actually been the donor; but, fortunately for her, Miss Pember was on another trail.

"Now, Blanche, tell us something else, please, Is it true that it was you who saw Dorothy throwing a certain letter—or piece of a letter—over the banisters into the hall?"

"Yes, Miss Pember."

Blanche had no hesitation in answering that apparently harmless question.

"Did you know what the paper was?"

"No."

"Do you know why she did it?"

"Oh, yes, Miss Pember. Rita told her to!"

"*Rita told her to!*" Miss Pember repeated, in a voice of stupefaction. And Blanche suddenly turned very white again, and gasped out:

"Oh—I oughtn't to have said that!"

"Never mind. You have said it now," Miss Pember told her sharply, and Blanche shivered where she stood.

Miss Chilcott, who was nearly as pale as the child, took a torn sheet of letter paper from her locked desk.

"I—suppose you don't know anything about this letter? Dorothy has owned that she wrote it. You need not be afraid of doing her any harm in that way."

Blanche looked at it with large surprised eyes.

"Why—it's the page she lost!" she said.

"What do *you* know about it? Miss Pember struck in sharply.

"She told me that she had lost it. She asked if I had seen it."

"Did she tell you what was written on it?"

"No. She only said that it was a piece of her story."

"A *what?*" Miss Chilcott and Miss Pember exclaimed together.

"A piece of her story," Blanche repeated, staring in wonder at their extraordinary expressions. "Didn't you know that Dorothy writes stories? Oh, yes! I didn't know till—till I was rather miserable one day and she read me a bit of one. It was *lovely.*"

Miss Chilcott and Miss Pember, with the paper between them, were reading the letter over again. Miss Chilcott turned suddenly and rang the bell.

"Please ask Miss Grayling to come down here at once!"

In the brief pause that followed, nobody said anything. All eyes were turned on the door waiting for Dorothy, who came in very pale and red-eyed.

"Dorothy—I am told that this letter is part of a story that you are writing?"

"Yes, Miss Pember!"

Dorothy looked, bewildered, from one face to another, and suddenly her white cheeks turned crimson.

"You didn't think it was a *real* letter?" she cried with a little gasp. "Oh—you *couldn't* think that?"

"What else was I to think?" asked Miss Chilcott slowly.

"May I see it, please? *Oh!*"

Dorothy hastily ran down the page and looked up with eyes full of tears.

"Oh—you didn't really think that I could have written like that of *my mother?*" she sobbed.

There was an extraordinarily uncomfortable pause.

"Please, *please* let me show you the rest of it, so that you may see I'm speaking the truth!" Dorothy cried earnestly. "Blanche knows where it is. May she go and fetch it?"

Miss Chilcott nodded, and Blanche eagerly ran.

"I'm afraid you'll think it awfully silly. *Please* don't read more of it than you must!" Dorothy besought. "The letter—the bit you read—is supposed to be written by a horrid girl—I made her just as horrid as I could—but she *does* get punished all right in the end!"

Miss Pember turned suddenly and stared out of the window, and Dorothy observed with surprise that her shoulders shook.

Miss Chilcott, who was less easily amused, waited patiently for the manuscript that Blanche brought a minute later.

"Is it a school story?" she inquired, taking it.

"Oh, no, Miss Chilcott!" said Dorothy, rather affronted. "It's quite a grown-up one. I don't care for writing school stories!"

Nothing could have been easier than to make sure—without hurting the feelings of the authoress by reading very much—that the suspicious page was an extract from the book. Dorothy's good memory had served her well. The second copy of the letter—signed "Your devoted Albinia,"—was almost word for word the same as its first edition.

"Dorothy, I understand, and—and I beg your pardon," said Miss Chilcott, with a long breath of relief. "You are quite right. I ought to have known perfectly well that you *could* not write a real letter like that."

"Need we keep Blanche any longer?" Miss Pember asked impatiently. She was fidgeting with an envelope in her hand.

"No. Blanche, you may go—and Dorothy with you," said Miss Chilcott.

"Back—to my room, Miss Chilcott?" Dorothy faltered.

Miss Chilcott smiled at her very kindly.

"No, my dear. But I think perhaps you had better keep away from the rest of the school till I have had time to straighten things out a little more. Suppose you go and do your lying-down in the drawing-room?"

"Yes, please, Miss Chilcott," said Dorothy thankfully. She couldn't have faced other girls just now—not with those red eyes, and the whole matter still so far from cleared up.

"Now—for the worst of it!" said Miss Chilcott, when they had gone, with a long breath.

"For Rita, you mean? Quite so!" said Miss Pember, and rang the bell sharply. "And—before she comes—just look at this, will you?"

"The silhouette that you did of her the other day?" said Miss Chilcott, looking with a weary wonder.

"No—the silhouette that I did of Anita Lyon, more than two years ago!"

"*What?* Impossible!"

"Here is Rita's. Look at the two together!" said Miss Pember, opening her envelope again.

Miss Chilcott stood looking in a dazed silence, for the two silhouettes were almost identical.

"But—"

"Yes, I know! It's incredible, isn't it? But think how much more often one sees a person's full face than the side face! The colouring, of course, is entirely different and the eyes and the hair. When one remembers Anita's fiery fuzz and her little bright greeny-grey eyes—"

The door opened, slowly and decorously, and both mistresses turned to face jet-black hair and slow black eyes, with no expression in them at all.

"Yes, Miss Chilcott? You sent for me?" said Rita.

NO. I don't mind telling you at all, now that I know the game is up," said Rita amiably, some very uncomfortable ten minutes later. "In fact, I'd like to. I'm rather proud of it! You'll expel me, of course; but that doesn't matter much. I'm eighteen, and I should have left anyhow at the end of the summer term."

Miss Chilcott and Miss Pember gazed at her in silence, words apparently failing them.

"Anita Lyon is my cousin and my greatest friend. She was simply furious when you expelled her—you knew that, of course. She said she let you see it pretty plainly. But she wasn't any more angry than I was, for her. We talked it over, of course, as soon as she came home, and I promised I'd do anything I could. It was rather difficult for her, you see, as she had to keep away from here.

"I got my father to send me to St. Madern's—I'd only been at a day-school before—and I made my plans. It was really very easy, just getting hold of a few girls and making them do what I wanted. Most girls are either silly or stupid. I reckoned on their never seeing what I was driving at till it was done, and by that time they'd be too much afraid of me to tell."

"Why were they afraid of you?" Miss Pember struck in abruptly.

"Well—most girls do things they shouldn't sometimes," said Rita, with an amiable smile. "I invented a sort of Secret Society—they all liked that—and got them to break a rule or two: and then it was easy enough, because they were afraid I'd report them. Blanche Bates, for instance—such a little pig! She'd do anything for a few sweets. And Hester Pyke: I caught her poking into someone's desk one day and counting money in a purse from it, and after that *she* did all I wanted. And Winifred Ray is a coward, and so good-natured and so silly. It never struck her what a serious thing it was to post letters for me, till after she'd done it. I pointed it out to her then, of course, but I never thought she'd be frightened enough to run away—I didn't think she had the courage for that. It was rather upsetting."

Rita paused for a moment, considering.

"I didn't quite realise *how* silly she was," she remarked. "A girl with any sense would have made sure of catching the postman, as I told her to, and if she missed doing that, she would have waited till the next day and not run a mile in the dark to a letter-box."

"Apparently you made her *too* much afraid of you," Miss Pember remarked drily.

"Yes; I suppose that was it," Rita agreed, with perfect amiability.

"Was Winifred your only letter-carrier?"

"Oh, no! Anita sent me what I wanted by post, of course, and I got someone to stop the postman on his way up to the house and get my parcel from him. That was why Blanche was out in the rain that afternoon."

"But she brought no parcel in with her?"

"Oh, no! There was rather a jolly hiding-place in the tool-shed, behind some flower-pots that were never moved, and I went and got my things whenever it fitted in. It was quite easy."

"Then I conclude that the Turkish Delight in Blanche's attaché-case was her wages for that errand?"

"Yes," Rita nodded. "That was why she was so keen to have it brought upstairs—for fear someone might open it. She was rather clumsy about the whole thing that night. I had to speak to her pretty sharply—she'd done it better before."

"So your materials for the feast of which we heard were sent to you in private parcels?"

Rita smiled.

"Some of them; but it was rather risky and I didn't like to trust to that too much. I brought back a good deal with me at the beginning of term, of course—things that would keep, like chocolates and nuts and crystallised fruits, and that didn't take up too much room in my drawers. ... You remember that I had a dressing-gown sent me?"

"From your old Aunt Susan!" Miss Pember supplied sharply.

Rita smiled at her.

"I haven't got an old Aunt Susan. Anita sent me the dressing-gown and a couple of books to account for the heaviness of the box. All the other things I wanted were packed underneath."

"And was your feast confined to the members of your Secret Society?"

"Oh, of course!"

"May one ask how you chose the members?"

"Of course!" said Rita again. "I told you that I'd tell anything you wanted to know. Besides, I'm really rather proud of that. You see, I only wanted a few girls, and I didn't want them all from one part of the school: just one here and one there, like—like *yeast*. It worried me rather how to pick them out, and then I suddenly thought of my own name."

"Your own name!"

"Yes. Perhaps you never thought—I hadn't, till then—how many surnames are the names of fish. Salmon, you see, and Fish itself, and Haddock, and so on. I thought it would be quite a good plan to let the Society arrange itself, like that, just by pure chance, and then no one could possibly guess how they were chosen, or why. It worked very well. Dorothy Grayling, Ada Ling, Winifred Ray, Ella Bass, Hester Pyke, Blanche Bates."

"Blanche Bates?" Miss Chilcott repeated, in a faint voice of bewilderment.

"Yes. Don't you see? *Whitebait!*" said Rita, with (as Miss Pember afterwards said savagely) her intolerable smile. "It was the Society of the Fish Girls—but I didn't tell them that, of course. We called it the F.G. I was the only person who knew more than that."

"Did they never ask?"

"Oh, yes, one or two of them did—*once*," said Rita, smiling meditatively.

"What was that extraordinary notice that I once saw on the Notice Board?" asked Miss Pember sharply.

"Did you really see one of my notices? That was very careless of me!" said Rita self-reproachfully. "I thought I had always taken them down before anyone except girls passed that way."

"I only saw it hurriedly, one morning early, when somebody cut a finger and I was sent for in a hurry. You needn't reproach yourself," said Miss Pember drily. "I had not time to look at it then, and it was gone before I came back. I supposed it was some silly joke."

Miss Chilcott, who had hardly spoken at all, cleared her throat and asked a question.

"Why did you do all this, Rita?"

"I told you, Miss Chilcott. For Anita!"

"Do you mean that, because your cousin had been expelled, you were deliberately trying to wreck the school?"

"Yes, Miss Chilcott," said Rita, looking up unabashed.

"And you never cared how miserable and frightened you made perfectly innocent girls?"

"I would have done it another way if I could, but there didn't seem to *be* any other way," said Rita, with a tinge of regret in her voice. "St. Madern's is such a jolly school! No one would ever have wanted to leave, unless I had made it a little unpleasant for them!"

"*A little unpleasant!*" Miss Pember exclaimed, under her breath.

"And is that why Cecily Carter left, and Florence Barbell, and Ruth Fish?"

"Yes, Miss Chilcott—and Joan Eeles. They were all members of the Fish Girls. You see, it was quite easy to get enough! Of course," said Rita reminiscently, "I didn't exactly *encourage* anybody to send girls here, if they spoke to me about it in the holidays, but that was a little more difficult—as I was staying on here myself."

There was a pause.

"I did think," said Rita regretfully, "that I had nearly finished my job—"

"And the school!" Miss Pember put in drily.

"And the school," Rita agreed placidly. "I hadn't much more time to waste, you see, with only one term beyond this. But, when I found that Winifred was leaving and Ella, I did think—"

She paused to sigh.

"I really should have done it, if it hadn't been for Dorothy Grayling; but there was no getting hold of her, in any way!"

"Do you know how that was, Rita?"

Rita looked up again, with an expression of perfect candour.

"Oh, yes!" she said, in a voice of surprise. "She is perfectly straight, and she isn't afraid of anything in the world except doing what she thinks wrong. You *can't* get hold of a person like that!"

Miss Chilcott and Miss Pember flashed an amazed glance at each other. It was Miss Chilcott who spoke.

"Rita," she said gently, "if you can see and understand that, how *can* you behave as you have been behaving?"

"Why—for Anita, of course!" said Rita, looking up again with that glance of perfect candour. "You don't suppose I *liked* doing it? But I would do anything for Anita!"

Both mistresses looked at her silently, Miss Chilcott with pure horror, but on the face of Miss Pember there was a very curious expression indeed.

"Is there anything else that you want to ask?" Rita inquired with perfect patience and politeness.

"I—don't think so," Miss Chilcott murmured slowly.

"Then—I'm expelled, of course? Yes, I knew that I would be," said Rita placidly. "Then please may I telephone to my father? I shall be glad to go at once, of course, and I don't suppose you want me to stay longer than I must."

Taking assent for granted, she moved quietly to Miss Chilcott's desk, and put through a trunk call in the most business-like and collected fashion.

"Is that Sir Isaac Salmon himself? Yes, father, Rita speaking. Will you please send the car for me at once? … Oh, I'm expelled! … Didn't you hear? E-x-p-e-l-l-e-d. … No, it is quite useless for you to come down yourself and talk it over, they are quite right about it. … *No*, thank you. I don't *want* you to come! … Very well, then I'll go and pack at once."

"May I go, Miss Chilcott?"

"Yes, Rita," Miss Chilcott answered mechanically.

Rita moved to the door, and then suddenly turned.

"There was one thing I forgot to tell you. About the mumps."

"About the *mumps!*"

"Yes. I got it from Anita."

"You *got it from Anita!*" Miss Chilcott gasped.

"Yes, Miss Chilcott. At the end of the Christmas holidays we heard that she had caught it, and of course I was supposed not to go and see her."

Rita paused a moment.

"Please don't blame my father, or think that he was cheating when he signed my health certificate. He never knew that I went."

"But you did go?"

"Oh, yes! It seemed such a good chance, for I had never had it and it's so terribly infectious—and I knew it would upset the whole term, if I could once get it going here. And, of course, it did."

"Not so very much. I think we have carried on pretty well," said Miss Pember grimly.

"No, not so *very* much," Rita agreed, with regret, and then added, brightening: "But, of course there is another batch due next week!"

Miss Pember gazed at her in a stony manner. Miss Chilcott appeared to have no words left.

"I may go and pack now, mayn't I?" said Rita mildly, and without waiting for an answer she walked out of the room and gently closed the door behind her.

"What an *awful* girl!" Miss Chilcott gasped faintly, finding her voice at last.

"She's a very remarkable girl," Miss Pember responded, suddenly and sharply. "And—I'm not sure that I ever came so near to liking her!"

"To *liking* her!" cried poor Miss Chilcott, as if she could not believe her ears.

"Yes. Oh, I'm not arguing for a moment that she hasn't behaved most abominably, for she has! But loyalty is a very rare virtue, Amy, and she has been absolutely and entirely—and most mistakenly, of course—loyal to her friend, at considerable cost to herself. She gets nothing out of it whatever, except the disgrace of being expelled; and it isn't everyone who would deliberately let herself in for a very painful and disfiguring complaint just to please a cousin."

Miss Chilcott only gazed at her in silent wonder.

"Yes! Rita is a very remarkable girl!" Miss Pember repeated, more sharply than ever. "If she gets into good hands, she may do almost anything. But—"

She suddenly tore the silhouettes into pieces, across and across.

"But I wish Anita had been *drowned* instead of expelled, two years ago!"

CHAPTER XIX

The Surprising Behaviour of Pills

"YOU will have to speak to the whole school," said Miss Pember to Miss Chilcott, when Rita, cool to the last, had whisked down the avenue in her father's magnificent car.

"I *know!*" Miss Chilcott murmured distressfully.

"And to Dorothy. And to those other five silly girls by themselves."

"I—I *can't!*" said Miss Chilcott, with a face of despair.

"Well, *I* can, if you like," said Miss Pember, looking as if she rather enjoyed the prospect.

"If only you would!"

"Not the school, of course. You are the head mistress. No one else can do that."

"No. I suppose not," Miss Chilcott agreed sadly.

"And Dorothy would not feel that it was at all the same thing if anyone but you spoke to *her.*"

"No. … I don't mind that part of it," said Miss Chilcott.

"Very well, then!" said Miss Pember, getting up with an air of battle. "Dorothy is still in the drawing-room, isn't she? You go and tackle her now; and I'll send for those *idiots*. And directly afterwards we'll summon the whole school and get it over."

Miss Chilcott perceptibly shivered.

"Cheer up, Amy! It will all be done within an hour," said Miss Pember. "And then let us hope that we may all settle down again and go on as if this wretched business had never been."

Miss Chilcott looked like anything but cheering up as she went slowly away to the drawing-room. But Miss Pember, remaining in the office, rang the bell and sent out her summons with a cheerful briskness.

"Please tell these five girls to come to me here at once: Miss Ray, Miss Pyke, Miss Ling, little Miss Bates, and Miss Bass."

The five girls came, singly, from different directions, and when they found themselves assembled, their faces expressed in different manners the liveliest emotions. They looked from one to another, and they knew that they were found out.

"No—you needn't look round for anyone else!" said Miss Pember crisply. "There are no more to come. Miss Chilcott is speaking to Dorothy by herself—*she* is on quite a different footing from the rest of you. And Rita has gone. She has been expelled."

Her sharp look, running from one to another, told her at once that the news surprised no one.

"What! you knew that, did you? So I suppose Hester was hanging out of some window, or prying from behind some door, as usual!"

Hester Pyke turned a lively crimson, and the other four looked more than a little foolish.

"Well! You needn't have troubled to do that, Hester," said Miss Pember, "for you would have heard soon enough. Yes, Rita is expelled, and your precious Secret Society has come to an end. ... Oh, yes, Miss Chilcott and I know all about it—even more than you do, perhaps, for *we* know what F.G. stands for! Do you?"

There was a faint and shamefaced murmur of "No, Miss Pember. ... No, Miss Pember."

"Fish Girls!" Miss Pember snapped at them. "Your surnames. Do you see? If you don't see, I am not going to trouble about explaining now—you can think it over for yourselves, and ask me some other time if you're too dense to make it out. But just now I have something else to say."

She looked sharply round again.

"You must have had a very miserable time, you more than foolish girls!" she said. "But it's over now—for good. You are not going to be punished any more; Miss Chilcott thinks that you have probably gone through enough already, in one way and another. We know, of course, that Rita was at the bottom of it all and that very much of the most of the blame was hers, but here's something for you all to think over. ... If you five had not been weak, or silly, or rule-breakers—or all three—you would never have got into Rita's power as you did, and she could never have got you into this mess."

She paused a moment, to let her remarks soak well in.

"And now—is St. Madern's going to be itself again?" she said, looking from one to another.

A very subdued murmur answered her, punctuated by sobs.

"Don't cry, Winifred! That will do no good at all," said Miss Pember. "It does seem a pity, doesn't it?—now that Rita has gone and the Society of the F.G. is dead—that you should be leaving at the end of the term."

"I don't *want* to leave—now!" Winifred answered, with tears.

"Nor do I!" Ellas Bass chimed in, in her sullen fashion.

"Then it was only Rita and her influence that made you want it at all?"

"Ye—yes!" sobbed Winifred. "I—I *love* St. Madern's! I shall never like any other—any other school half as we—ell!"

Ella, meeting Miss Pember's eye, nodded a sulky assent.

"I—see!" said Miss Pember slowly. "Well—it does indeed seem a pity then, doesn't it?"

"Oh, Miss Pember! Can't we stay?" Winifred wept, in the depths of woe.

"I don't know about that at all, Winifred," Miss Pember answered her seriously. "*You* may not want, now, to leave St. Madern's. But the question remains—does St. Madern's want to keep you? I am quite sure that none of you *meant* to do harm to the school, but the harm has been done, and—well, as I say, I don't know!"

Winifred's ready tears were by this time flowing in a perfect river, and even the sullen Ella was suspiciously red and choking a little. Miss Pember, who hated sentiment, rose in a hurry.

"That will do—that will do!" she said hastily. "It's quite useless in any case to make an object of yourself, Winifred. For goodness' sake go and get a clean handkerchief—*two* clean handkerchiefs if you can't stop crying! Hester, you are the senior girl here. Please go and ask Phyllis to give out a notice that Miss Chilcott wants the whole school in the hall at once."

The sad remnant of the Secret Society of the Fish Girls melted forlornly away, and Miss Pember beckoned briskly to Miss Chilcott: who, coming out of the drawing-room at that precise moment, was waiting in an agitated manner for them to get out of sight before she came forward.

"It's all right, Amy!" said Miss Pember. "Gas and gaiters, and tears, and a complete surrender—even Ella reduced to a sniffing misery. What about Dorothy?"

"Dorothy is a perfect dear!" said Miss Chilcott with emotion.

"*That's* all right!" said Miss Pember, cutting her very short. "Now, for goodness gracious sake, Amy, don't *you* begin to weep, for you've got to pull yourself together and address the school!"

"I—*can't!*" gasped Miss Chilcott forlornly.

"*Got* to!" said Miss Pember. "Come along now, and get it over—and make it as short as you like!"

She hauled her reluctant head mistress along the passages by sheer force of energy; but at the very door of the hall, with her hand on the handle, she most abruptly paused.

"Wait! There's something going on there already!" she said.

Miss Chilcott very thankfully waited, and Miss Pember, softly opening the door, beckoned her to come nearer. They saw a truly amazing sight.

The whole school was gathered in the hall, according to instructions; so absorbed that not a girl noticed the gentle opening of the door, or was aware of the two additional listeners. On the platform, by Miss Chilcott's sacred desk, stood—of all people in the world—Phyllis Wills, Pills, the Captain of the School, who had no influence and of whom nobody ever thought twice. But they were all listening to her now with a vengeance, so quietly that the little weak voice of Pills carried without difficulty all over the big room.

"—all ashamed of ourselves," she was saying. "A whole lot of people must have known that something was wrong with the school. *I* didn't. I never knew anything. I ought never to have been Captain. I'm no good at all—except at lessons. I'm sorry. I'm ashamed of myself. But you *knew* that I wasn't any good; and some of you other people who did know ought to have done something. We've let the school down. We ought to be ashamed of ourselves—"

("I always *knew* that Pills would be the worst speaker in the world!" Miss Pember murmured softly, outside the door.

"Pills?" Miss Chilcott murmured vaguely back.

"Surely you knew that she was called that? Oh, *Amy*—Hush—she's going on.")

Pills, who had been very elaborately blowing her nose, resumed her discourse.

"We've let the school down—oh, I said that before! We've got to pull it up again. We've made Miss Chilcott miserable, and you all know quite well that that makes her ill—and we're all most awfully fond of her, really, aren't we?"

A cordial murmur rippled round the silent room and died away again.

("Don't, Amy—*don't!*" Miss Pember murmured urgently. "Here—here's my handkerchief, if you've lost yours!")

"It's an awful thing for a school," said Pills, "to have two girls expelled. We've got to pull up the school again. We've got to get new girls to come. But the real thing is, that each of us has got to—to behave most frightfully decently from now on without stopping. ... Because if you can't trust people, a school must—must go to pot. And it's up to *each* of us—not to the whole lot in a bunch. And a school is no stronger than its weakest link—no, that's wrong. It's a chain, of course, but you know what I mean. And we all ought to be ashamed of ourselves—"

"Oh, I really can't bear to hear that any *more!*" said Miss Pember, with a little gasp that was partly irritation and partly laughter, and partly something very different. "*Dear* Pills! I never knew before that I liked her so much—but she really *is* the worst speaker in the world!"

She pushed open the door, and the listening girls, turning at last, saw who had been standing outside. A little murmur of dismay went round the hall, and Pills, turning the colour of a beetroot, stumbled owlishly off the platform, missed a step and came to the ground in a most ungraceful manner.

"Hurt yourself? No? *That's* all right!" said Miss Pember, rapidly passing her, and was up in her place in a twinkling.

"Girls—there's hardly anything to say to you, because Phyllis has said it all already, and Miss Chilcott—who is a little upset and was very much dreading having to speak to you—is very much obliged to her. You know that Rita Salmon has been expelled, and you know that Dorothy Grayling was accused of all sorts of things which were quite untrue. Well! That's all over, and we will forget it as fast as we can, and just devote ourselves to making St. Madern's once again what it used to be: only remembering, as Phyllis most justly reminded us, that a chain is no stronger than its weakest link, and it is up to each one of us to make sure that our own particular link is a strong one in the St. Madern's chain. That's all. You may go."

"And I really think," said Miss Pember pungently to Miss Chilcott, "that the girls look happier already! It's astonishing how far one bad influence can spread. Though Winifred's eyes are the colour of tomatoes, she is quite cheerful; and I never saw Ella less sulky."

"I wish they weren't going," Miss Chilcott lamented.

"If you really mean that," said Miss Pember, "they *shan't* go!"

And, as a matter of fact, they did not. Ella was permitted to arrange the matter with her own people as she pleased. But Miss Pember actually took her courage in her hand and went up to London to interview Winifred's terrible father, returning shaken but victorious.

"An awful man! I really thought at one time that I was going to be beaten," she confessed frankly to Miss Chilcott. "I'm not going to tell you, my dear, all the things he said about our having such a girl as Rita in the school at all—as if anyone could tell what she was like by just looking at her! But I wore him down at last, when I had let him bellow as much as he liked; and Winifred is to stay."

"I am very glad of that. I like Winifred," said Miss Chilcott.

"So do I," said Miss Pember. "But she will have to learn to grow a backbone for herself, if she doesn't want to get into this sort of trouble all through her life. There are more Ritas than one in the world."

"Oh, I hope not!" said Miss Chilcott fervently.

"Not here, at any rate. *One* of the breed has been almost enough to kill St. Madern's," said Miss Pember. "Now—I'm late for rehearsal as it is, and I can't afford to waste another minute!"

"Let the rehearsal go for to-day. You are so tired," Miss Chilcott urged.

"Nonsense! *I'm* no weakling, at any rate!" said Miss Pember vigorously. And she went off to play Hermia to Dorothy's Helena, as vigorously as if she had been sitting in an arm-chair all the morning, returning to report great success to Miss Chilcott.

"The best rehearsal we have ever had! … Yes, *of course* I'm going to play Hermia in the play. Why not? … Don't *make* difficulties, Amy. There's no one else in the least suitable, and can you give me any good reason why I should *not* act with the girls? Do be happy, and rejoice that your troubles are over. Rita gone, nobody else leaving, the school beginning to feel like its old self—"

"And no more mumps," murmured Miss Chilcott.

"*And,*" said Miss Pember energetically, "what is infinitely more important—no more of the F.G.!"

Books to Treasure

Old favourites

E M Channon:
Expelled from School
Her Second Chance (forthcoming)

Dorothea Moore:
A Runaway Princess (eBook only)
Brenda of Beech House (eBook only)
Wanted: an English Girl (forthcoming)

Evelyn Smith:
Queen Anne series
Seven Sisters at Queen Anne's
Septima at School
Phyllida in Form III

The First Fifth Form
The Small Sixth Form

New favourites to discover

PICTURE BOOKS
HELEN BARBER:
The Princess and the Socks

ALI OXTOBY:
Hens in High Heels (forthcoming)

MARIANNE DE PIERRES:
Serious Sas and Messy Magda

A J WEAVER:
Be Quiet, Bird!
Big Cats, Little Cats

EARLY READERS
Ali Oxtoby
Pete's Penguin (forthcoming)

YOUNG ADULT
Phillip Davies
Destiny's Rebel (forthcoming)

Eleanor Watkins
The Village (forthcoming)

sales@bookdragonbooks.co.uk   www.bookdragonbooks.co.uk